RISING FROM THE RUINS

A Story of Restoration and Healing

Mary Cross

Grammabooks & Events LLC

To my dear husband, family, and friends—
Thank you for your steadfast love, encouragement, and belief in
me throughout this journey.

And to the rebuilders—those who rise, piece by piece, from what
was broken— May your faith be greater than the ruins behind
you.

"They will rebuild the ancient ruins and restore the places long
devastated." — Isaiah 61:4

CONTENTS

CRACKS IN THE FOUNDATION

The sunlight filtered dimly through the bookstore's dusty windows, casting fragmented light onto the small table where Logan and Drew sat. Logan's grip tightened around the worn handle of his coffee mug, the sharp clink of porcelain breaking the silence. Drew worked quietly a few feet away, unpacking a shipment of books, his sleeves rolled up to reveal forearms dusted with cardboard flecks. He didn't look up as Logan muttered, "Lost another one."

"What happened this time?" Drew asked, his voice low and steady. He never pried, but Logan had been showing up regularly since he was fired from his last job. The pattern was becoming familiar.

Logan shrugged, leaning back in his chair. "Same as always. Tempers flared. Mine, mostly. It's like... yelling and screaming are all I know."

Drew paused in his unpacking, straightening as he looked up. His brow furrowed in quiet concern. "You've said that before. Where does that come from?"

Logan hesitated. Drew's words stirred memories Logan tried to avoid, but they always found a way in—faint echoes of harsh words and the dim flicker of a kitchen bulb creeping into his thoughts. His grip on the coffee mug tightened further; his gaze fixed on a crack in the table.

The kitchen was small, lit by the harsh glow of a single bulb that flickered sporadically. Nineteen-year-old Logan stood at the counter, arranging roasted chicken on a serving plate with deliberate care. "I made broccoli for us, Mom," he said, setting the plate down on the table.

He loved his mom. She had learned to keep the peace by keeping quiet. If she challenged his stepfather, the yelling turned on her instead. Logan didn't see her as weak—just worn down. But love wasn't enough to make him stay.

"But don't worry—I cooked carrots for him. You know how much he loves broccoli."
His tone carried a faint smirk, and his mother gave him a tired smile, her eyes softening briefly despite her exhaustion. The aroma of the meal filled the air, lending a rare sense of warmth to the cramped space.

"Dinner smells wonderful, honey," she said softly, her voice warm as she prepared to take a bite.
"Thanks, Mom," Logan replied, a rare warmth in his voice. He'd been working double shifts at the diner downtown, saving every penny so he could finally leave this house. Tonight, he wanted to make something nice—something that felt like a small victory.

"You've been working so hard lately," his mother added gently. "I know you're saving to leave, but... give it a little more time? Just until you have a little more cushion?"

Logan hesitated, glancing at her. "I've already got a plan. I just need to make it another month or so."

The front door slammed, shattering the fleeting sense of peace. Heavy boots thudded on the linoleum—each step sharp and deliberate, like a warning. His stepfather strode into the kitchen, the air shifting with his presence.

"What's this?" his stepfather grunted, eyeing the table.

"Dinner," Logan said, forcing his voice to stay even.

His stepfather sat down heavily, stabbing at the roasted chicken with his fork. He took a bite, then shoved the plate an inch forward.

"Chicken's fine," he spat, his voice already climbing. "But what's with the broccoli? You know I hate that."

Logan's hand tightened on the countertop.
"It's for Mom. She likes it," he said, his tone deliberately calm but tinged with defiance.

"So, you knew I don't like broccoli, but you made it anyway? For you and your mother?"

His stepfather's voice cracked like a whip, sharp and deliberate. He leaned in, eyes narrowing.

"What are you up to, boy? You think this is your house now? That you're in charge?"

He jabbed his fork at Logan, his hand trembling with anger.
"I come home, and this is the respect I get? A dinner that's nothing but a slap in the face?"

He threw the fork onto the plate. The clatter made Logan flinch.

"You think you're some kind of hero, helping your mother out with a meal now and then? Let me tell you something, boy—doing the bare minimum doesn't make you special. You're just a lazy kid who's too full of himself to see how the real world works. And believe me, it's no picnic out there."

The words pounded against Logan's ears, each one landing like a blow. He glanced at his mother, who stared down at her plate, her fingers gripping the fork tightly, as if it could anchor her in place. She had remarried to give them both a chance at stability— but now, watching her son's face harden with anger, she couldn't escape the regret.

"Enough!" Logan roared, slamming his hands on the counter. The room fell silent, his mother staring wide-eyed at him, his stepfather frozen in surprise.

"I'm done," Logan said, his voice trembling but firm. "I've done everything I can to make this place livable, to help Mom, and it's never enough for you. I'm leaving."

As Logan moved toward the door, his mother's voice broke the silence.

"Logan, please..." She rose slightly from her chair as if to follow him, but she hesitated, casting a glance toward her husband. Slowly, she sank back down, the weight of her decision keeping her rooted in place.

"Fine. Leave!" his stepfather shouted, his voice cold and final. "And don't come crawling back when the world spits you out."

Logan didn't wait for the rest. He turned and walked out, the weight of years of anger and frustration finally breaking free. Relief swelled with every step, but guilt clung to him like an unyielding shadow. The memory of his mother's plea—and the way she sank back into her chair—stayed with him, rooting itself deep in his mind: a constant reminder of what he couldn't escape.

Drew's voice pulled Logan back to the present.

"It's not an excuse," Logan said quickly. "I'm an adult. I should be able to control it by now. But every time someone pushes the wrong button... it's like I'm back there, reliving it all over again."

Drew's hands hovered over the stack of books for a moment. He thrived on tasks like this, where things came together under his control. But people were messy. Drew glanced at Logan, recognizing the jagged edges of someone trying to piece himself back together.

"Maybe this community center project could help," Drew said finally. "You remind me of someone who thought anger was all he had left. Turns out, he was wrong. Building something helped him see things differently. It might help you too."

Logan snorted. "Me? Building something with a group of people? I'm not exactly a team player."

"Neither am I," Drew admitted. "But sometimes, working together can surprise you. At least think about it."

Logan didn't respond immediately, his mind drifting back to the crumpled flyer Drew had handed him a week ago:

Volunteers Needed for Community Center Rehab

He still wasn't sure why he hadn't tossed it. Maybe it was the way Drew always seemed steady, like a quiet anchor in the middle of chaos. Logan didn't trust many people, but something about Drew made him feel... less alone.

"Maybe I'll show up," he muttered, folding the flyer and shoving it back into his jacket pocket. Small steps, he thought. One step could lead to something better. Perhaps building something that mattered could help him break free from the weight he'd been carrying for years.

As Logan tucked the flyer into his pocket, Drew glanced at the shelves around him. This wasn't the first time he'd seen a man trying to rebuild from the ruins of anger and loss. Drew had been there himself once, though in a different way. Logan's face reminded him of that same struggle: a man weighed down by burdens he didn't choose, fighting to hold onto hope.

A VISION WORTH BUILDING

Maiya ran her fingers along the worn spine of a paperback, but her mind wasn't in the bookstore. It was consumed by thoughts of a quiet, boarded-up building she had fantasized about for years—a building that was now under her name. The aroma of old books and floor polish hung in the air, keeping her grounded, while her thoughts raced with future plans.

Being the middle child of seven, Maiya had mastered the art of self-reliance from an early age. Her older siblings moved on swiftly, leaving her to care for the younger ones who demanded constant attention. This positioned Maiya in the middle ground —never seeking the spotlight, never causing trouble, never requiring rescue. She simply existed, seldom drawing notice unless necessary.

She had learned to refrain from seeking attention—not because she didn't desire it, but because disappointment seemed more common than acknowledgment. Instead, she perfected the skill of blending into overlooked spaces.

Whether it was the secluded nooks of the library or the deserted property on the outskirts of her neighborhood, Maiya found solace in these forgotten places.

Even now, she could vividly recall riding her bike past the building as a child, gazing at the boarded-up windows, weathered paint, and vines snaking over the foundation. Adults had discussed it within earshot—the city had intentions of transforming it into a community center, but funding ran dry before completion. Over time, conversations about it faded. Yet, the building stood, waiting.

Even in her youth, she envisioned its potential.

She imagined children streaming through the doors, families congregating, individuals discovering a sense of belonging. And even years later, that vision never left her. Now, that dream was within her grasp to materialize.

Maiya was naturally drawn to places—and people—that went unnoticed. This inclination led her to a career in the nonprofit sector.

After college, she dedicated herself to helping others bring their aspirations to life. Her work transcended mere fundraising; it was about constructing something enduring. One successful grant led to another, and soon she had built a thriving career collaborating with local shelters, after-school programs, and community projects—securing funding that translated ideas into reality.

She had accumulated significant financial savings over the years without a clear destination—until an opportunity presented itself.

One evening, while reviewing upcoming funding prospects, Maiya stumbled upon a public notice from the city. The abandoned property was up for sale, earmarked not for just anyone, but for someone willing to refurbish it and complete the long-forgotten community center project. She meticulously devised a strategic plan, outlining budgets, partnerships, and timelines. Once all the pieces fell into place, she made the purchase.

The childhood dream was now a tangible reality.

But when word spread of Maiya's property acquisition, not everyone offered support.

During a city planning meeting, she encountered Keith Ridelson, a seasoned business owner involved in local development for years. He was the type to offer firm handshakes, speak boisterously, and consistently find flaws in ideas.

As Maiya presented her renovation plans, Keith barely let her finish before smirking under his breath. A ripple of conversation traversed the room as he chuckled, perusing her proposal.

"This is quite ambitious," he remarked, shaking his head. "You might be taking on more than you can handle."

Leaning back, he tapped a finger on the documents. "Projects of this nature demand experience. Are you truly prepared to bear such responsibility?"

A few individuals shifted uneasily. A man coughed awkwardly, avoiding Maiya's gaze.

Encounters with men like Keith Ridelson were not new to Maiya —individuals who underestimated her. But she was acutely aware of her capabilities, and no amount of skepticism could sway her.

Her smile remained unwavering, though her grip on the folder under the table tightened. She had faced skeptics before, but something about Keith's condescension struck a chord. Still, she brushed aside the flicker of uncertainty. This was not the moment for doubt.

"Leadership isn't just about concrete pouring—it's about uniting the right people to accomplish the task," she responded calmly.

Keith exhaled sharply. "Well, time will tell how long you can keep up this façade."

That evening, the planning committee approved her proposal.

Early the next day, Maiya took to the streets, determined not to let Keith Ridelson dampen her spirit. She visited local establishments, putting up flyers soliciting volunteers and announcing an organizational gathering at the property that Saturday.

She knew the request was audacious—expecting commitment before the first nail was hammered in place. But she also knew this: if she didn't believe in the vision enough to ask others to join, no one else would.

Years of proving that change was possible had led her to this moment. Now, she had to persuade others that this vision was worth embracing.

DREW'S JOURNEY

Drew arranged a row of books on the shelf, his fingers lingering on the spines. The bookstore had become their sanctuary, their second chance—but lately, it felt as though something was missing. Over the years, the store had evolved into more than just a job. It was a cornerstone of his and Sarah's new life, a life they had reconstructed from the ground up.

He often caught glimpses of himself in the faces of customers lingering in the coffee area, their hands wrapped around warm mugs, their eyes scanning the shelves without urgency.

He recognized that restlessness—the quiet search for something they couldn't quite name. Lately, that same feeling had begun stirring in him again: a gentle nudge, like a whisper telling him there was something more.

Across the store, Sarah sat behind the counter, carefully sorting through a stack of new books. A faint hum escaped her lips as she worked, a song she probably didn't realize she was singing. Drew watched her for a moment, taking in the glow on her cheeks, the easy way she smiled now.

There had been a time when her smile was rare, her strength so diminished that Drew hadn't been sure what their future would hold.

Years earlier, before the bookstore, Drew had sat alone in the sanctuary. The wooden pews stretched before him, silent witnesses to the life he thought he'd always have. A blank notebook lay in his lap, its empty pages staring back at him like an unanswered prayer.

"Lord, give me the words."

The silence around him seemed to echo his uncertainty. This place had been his refuge for years—the backdrop for baptisms, weddings, and prayers shared over coffee and tears. Each memory felt like a goodbye he wasn't ready to say.

He thought of Sarah.

They met in seminary, their shared passion for ministry forging an immediate bond. Together, they co-pastored a growing church, pouring their hearts into shepherding a congregation that had become like family.

Everything had been going according to plan—until Sarah's illness changed everything.

At first, it was easy to dismiss her fatigue, her moments of weakness. They blamed stress, overwork, anything but what it was: a rare, chronic condition that would slowly erode her strength. The diagnosis shattered their carefully laid plans.

They prayed fervently for healing, pleading for a miracle. But the answer they received wasn't the one they had hoped for.

As Sarah's condition progressed, Drew realized he couldn't be both a full-time pastor and the husband she needed. The congregation deserved a leader who could give them everything—and Drew couldn't be that man anymore.

"God," he whispered, running a hand over the blank pages of his notebook, "I trust You, but I don't understand."

The words finally came—not about endings, but transitions. About trusting God in the unknown.

Later that week, Drew stood before the congregation, his voice steady despite the ache in his chest.

"This isn't goodbye," he told them. "This is a new path—one God has called us to walk together."

There were tears, hugs, and prayers. Words of understanding and encouragement. As Drew stepped away from the pulpit for the last time, he felt both loss and peace—a strange mix of sorrow and certainty that comes when you know you're following God's will, even without all the answers.

After stepping away from the ministry, Drew and Sarah found solace in the bookstore. What began as a temporary job to make ends meet soon became something far more meaningful. The work was practical, even mundane at times, but the rhythm of it brought comfort.

Together, they nurtured the little coffee area, transforming it into a haven for reflection and conversation. In time, Drew realized they hadn't stepped away from ministry at all—it had simply taken a different form.

An unexpected blessing emerged. Sarah's illness, which they had feared would progress rapidly, seemed to stabilize. It wasn't the miraculous healing they had prayed for, but it was a quiet mercy—a steady hand they hadn't expected but were deeply thankful for.

A few years after Drew took on the store manager position, the owner decided to retire and offered to sell it to them. Drew and Sarah prayed over the decision, and when they bought the bookstore, they saw it as a gift, not just a business.

Looking around the store now, Drew felt a deep peace settle over him. This wasn't the life they had planned, but it was the one God had prepared for them.

Still, something stirred in his spirit—a quiet sense that there was more waiting for him, just beyond his reach.

The bell above the door jingled, pulling Drew from his thoughts. He glanced up as Maiya walked in, her purposeful stride and warm smile lighting up the room. A brightly colored flyer was tucked under her arm.

FOUNDATIONS
OF PURPOSE

Maiya arrived at the community center early. The brilliant colors of sunrise had just begun to show through the newly washed front windows, softening the rough edges of the space that still smelled faintly of old paint and sawdust.

Her makeshift office in the corner of the main room had become a quiet command center—a donated table, mismatched chairs, a filing cabinet, her ever-present laptop, and the quiet hum of her assistant typing at a nearby desk. With restoration underway, supply orders piling up, and program planning beginning to demand real structure, the assistant had become essential for keeping things on track.

The heater kicked on with a thump as Maiya opened her notes and tried to focus.

This was the first real planning meeting that had nothing to do with reconstruction. It marked the beginning of operational planning for the long-awaited community center.

She had asked Drew and Sarah to come prepared with lists —what they believed the community center should offer, and what would be needed to make it happen. She wanted their perspectives, not just their support.

God, You've brought us this far. Help me hear what they see.

She looked up as Sarah wheeled herself in through the side door, a wool wrap tucked around her shoulders. A moment later, Drew stepped in behind her, carrying a small bakery bag and a coffee carrier.

"Breakfast meeting," he said, holding up the goods. "Figured we could use something warm to go with all this vision casting."

Sarah gave Maiya a warm smile. "You've been here awhile already, haven't you?"

Maiya shrugged. "Just getting things in order."

They settled in at the table, the rustle of paper mixing with the tap of keys as Maiya pulled up her notes. Her assistant had placed a single-page handout at each seat, a reference sheet listing common services offered at community centers. It included examples like after-school tutoring, senior lunches, parenting workshops, fitness classes, job skills training, and emotional support groups. The handouts weren't meant to define the vision, only to prompt ideas.

"Thanks again for coming. I know everyone's busy. I just thought it might help if we each brought a list of what we see this place becoming—and what it's going to take to get there."

Drew nodded and set a folded paper on the table. Sarah placed a small spiral notebook beside it.

Maiya went first.

She walked them through her outline: startup funding from a grant she was almost ready to submit, operating expenses for the first six months, a three-tiered program model based on similar centers she'd worked with.

"I know we can't launch everything at once," she added quickly, "but I wanted you to see where this could go. I've written grants for other centers. I started saving the best ideas years ago—just in case something like this ever happened."

Drew raised an eyebrow. "You've been planning this a long time."

Maiya offered a small smile. "Longer than I realized."

She glanced at the others, then leaned back slightly. "Okay, let's hear what you both see. I'm really curious how your perspectives compare."

Drew unfolded his notes and cleared his throat. His list was handwritten, folded into quarters, creased like it had lived in his jacket pocket for days.

"From what I've seen so far," he began, "teenagers need a place to go after school. Seniors are lonely. Parents are overwhelmed. And everyone seems to be waiting for someone else to step up."

He glanced at them. "We start small. Do the right things first. People won't trust the programs until they trust the people running them."

Maiya nodded slowly, her expression thoughtful. "That's true. When people have been overlooked or worn down by life, they're not looking for polished programs—they're looking for sincerity. You're right about teens, seniors, and parents. Each one carries weight most people don't see. If we can create a space where they're genuinely seen, heard, and valued... then we're not just running a center—we're restoring hope."

Sarah opened her notebook and said, "My list is simple, but it's foundational—just seven bullet points. Story-time corner. Rocking chair. Snacks. A few donated toys. A shelf with diapers and baby wipes. A tea kettle. A space to cry where no one asks questions."

She paused, then added softly, "And maybe a quiet corner for tutoring—kids falling behind need a place to catch up. And someone to help them believe they can."

Maiya nodded, adding it to her notes. "That's important. Honestly, I wouldn't have thought of some of this—but it fills in what I missed."

"We should probably think about transportation too," Drew added. "Even if we can't run a van right away, we need to know who can get here and who can't."

Maiya scribbled again. "Transportation... long-term goal. These are the gaps we'll miss unless we talk through it like this."

Before anyone could respond further, the front door creaked open.

Mitch stepped in, brushing the cold off his shoulders. He carried a clipboard and a thermos, his presence filling the doorway like he wasn't sure whether to stay or go.

"Thanks for the invite," he said, looking at Maiya. "Appreciate you thinking of me."

"Glad you could make it," she replied genuinely. "We're going over ideas for what the center will offer—and what it's going to take to make it work."

Mitch pulled up a chair, glancing at the scattered notes.

"You've got vision, spreadsheets, and snacks. Looks like you're on the right track." He gave a rare half-smile. "Here's a thought. What if we had a tool library? Folks could check out basic stuff for home repairs, maybe take a class or two. Teach some folks how to fix what's broken."

He leaned back, tapping the edge of his clipboard. "Could keep it simple—screen repair, window glazing, electrical safety. Maybe even set up small clinics by appointment. No big walk-ins, just a few at a time."

Drew leaned forward. "That would draw people in. Everyone

needs help fixing something."

Sarah nodded. "It gives them a reason to come. And a reason to come back. Speaking of clinics, if there is a need, we could look for volunteers to offer haircuts for people searching for jobs and work with area laundromats to clean donated clothing for job interviews."

Maiya jotted it down. "Okay. That's getting added." Then she looked up again, a slow smile spreading across her face. "I knew we'd all bring different perspectives—but seeing it like this... it's better than I imagined. Nothing overlaps, but every piece fits." She paused. "But before we start inviting people in, we need to think through safety."

Sarah nodded. "If we're going to have kids here—or really anyone vulnerable—we'll need to screen volunteers. Background checks, at minimum."

Drew added, "And we should be clear about where we need certified professionals. We can't let good intentions replace trained help. We also need to consider the safety of the people volunteering. That means security staffing."

"I'll add liability and insurance to the startup checklist," Maiya said. "And we'll need to define who's a volunteer and what roles might eventually require paid staff. As we identify staff members and their salary, we can start to get a better idea of budget needs. We'll need to determine an initial operating budget and what belongs on it."

Mitch spoke up again. "You might be able to write a grant that covers training or safety certifications. If you want the teaching piece to grow, you'll need structure behind it."

Maiya nodded. "There are a few grant lines for community skill-building. I'll look into what fits."

She paused, looking at each of them in turn.

"Let's plan the first volunteer interest meeting," she said. "Next Saturday?"

Drew nodded. "If even five people come, we'll know where to start."

Sarah added, "And they'll see we're serious. That matters."

"We're not going to be able to do this alone. Not even the four of us. I've been thinking about forming committees—small teams to take on different pieces: programs, facilities, volunteers, outreach, and fundraising."

She looked down at her notebook. "We can start by defining what each committee might be responsible for. Programs would handle class scheduling, supplies, and instructors. Facilities would track repairs, cleaning, and maintenance. Volunteers would recruit, screen, and schedule help. Outreach would manage communication—flyers, local events, maybe a newsletter. Fundraising would coordinate events and track donations."

Drew nodded. "We'll need committee leads. Just a few steady people willing to take ownership and follow through."

Sarah added, "And someone to check in with all of them so no one feels like they're running solo."

Mitch leaned back. "That's a lot of coordination. Good structure to build on, though. I'd be willing to help with the facilities side— just don't expect me to make posters."

"And maybe health and wellness," Sarah added. "Even just blood pressure checks or nutrition talks. Something simple to start."

Drew nodded thoughtfully. "Let people own part of it. That's how we make it last."

Sarah smiled faintly. "Feels like we're already building something."

They spent the next hour reviewing notes, revisiting earlier ideas, and prioritizing which pieces could be set in motion first. They mapped out short-term and long-term goals, drafted a preliminary list of volunteer roles, and discussed timelines for building access, room assignments, and storage needs. There were questions about which services would need legal or municipal review, and which ones could launch with simple oversight. They acknowledged the need for both structure and flexibility— something that could grow with the community but still start small enough to manage.

Before the meeting ended, Maiya made a checklist of key follow-up items: confirm liability insurance requirements, contact the city about zoning for specific program types, outline training guidelines for volunteers, and identify which grant lines could be submitted within the next thirty days. Everyone agreed that scheduling an open house or volunteer interest meeting would be the next milestone.

And just like that, the foundation of the center began to take shape—not with bricks or beams, but with plans, processes, and people willing to carry the vision forward.

As the others talked and scribbled ideas, Maiya sat quietly for a moment, soaking it in. This wasn't just planning anymore. This was real. It was happening. And she wasn't carrying it alone. She had dreamed alone for so long. But now, the dream was shared— and finally beginning to take on life.

BUILDING MOMENTUM

Drew entered the community center through the heavy double doors, met by the scent of sawdust and old paint. Despite the building's worn exterior, the neglect inside was undeniable. Sunlight filtered through boarded-up windows, exposing water-stained beams and peeling plaster. Yet, as Drew's eyes adjusted to the dim light, he could see the potential. The tired atmosphere reminded him of past projects he had rejuvenated—endeavors that had held significant value.

Maiya was already inside, clipboard in hand, projecting determination. "Good morning," she greeted, gesturing toward the open framework above them. "Allow me to demonstrate the challenges we're facing."

As they moved through the main hall, Maiya's footsteps echoed on the uneven floor, the air thick with a blend of lingering paint smells and the earthy aroma of aged wood. She pointed to a section of the roof where a temporary patch covered a sizable hole.

"The original HVAC installation was done improperly many years ago," Maiya explained. "This resulted in structural damage, which we're currently rectifying. Despite the temporary patch, the new system still needs installation."

Drew examined the exposed ducts attentively. "And the current HVAC company?"

Maiya sighed, flipping through her notes. "They've been evasive all week. They said they'd check their schedule, but then communication suddenly stopped. I left a voicemail yesterday, but haven't heard back."

Handing him two sets of documents, Maiya presented proposals from different HVAC vendors side by side. "Here's the breakdown. The first company offers a lower bid, but with reduced coverage. The second company conducted a thorough site evaluation, including necessary duct adjustments."

Seated at a folding table, Drew reviewed the proposals, tracing his thumb along the edges as he examined the figures and technical details. "The second company is charging $12,500 more," he noted. "However, they'll address additional duct work, replace outdated vents, and seal off problematic areas not covered by the first bid."

Peering over his shoulder, Maiya asked, "Is the extra cost justified?"

"Absolutely," Drew confirmed, tapping the papers for emphasis. "Cutting corners here would only lead to higher expenses in the long run. The second company has already proven their reliability."

"Good," Maiya stated decisively. "I'll reach out to them today to finalize the contract. With HVAC installation, mold remediation, and final inspections on the agenda, we need to avoid any delays."

Maiya led Drew to the far end of the building, where a section of flooring had been cordoned off with faded caution tape fluttering in the draft. "This area was flagged by the inspector," she explained. "Water collected here due to roof damage, resulting in structural complications. A professional remediation team is scheduled to arrive today."

Kneeling beside the restricted section, Drew ran his hand over a damp, dark beam. The wood felt soft, almost spongy. Scraping his fingernail across it, he dislodged flecks of mold, revealing a more extensive spread than anticipated, causing unease to stir in his stomach.

"You made the right call by bringing in professionals," Drew said, wiping his hand on his jeans. "Volunteers shouldn't handle this."

Maiya nodded. "Once they clear the mold and replace the beams, we can proceed. The replacement materials are already arranged, and the remediation team has guaranteed completion by tonight."

"Excellent plan," Drew agreed, standing and brushing off his hands. "There are plenty of other tasks for volunteers to tackle in the meantime."

The following morning, Drew parked his truck in the cracked lot adjacent to the community center. The air was crisp, hinting at rain, and the early morning sky displayed pale golden streaks. Glancing at his watch—it was 7:00 a.m.—even though the first volunteer shift wasn't set to start until 8:00, he wanted to inspect the site before the activities began.

Entering through the side door, he was greeted by the familiar scents of sawdust and fresh paint. Dust motes danced in the beams of sunlight filtering through the boarded windows. Across the room, Maiya stood at a folding table, focused on her clipboard. Her half-full coffee cup sat precariously close to a stack of paperwork.

"You're here early," she remarked, looking up with a slight smile.

Drew shrugged. "Not as early as you. I thought I'd acquaint myself with the place before it gets busy."

Maiya chuckled. "Good idea." Pointing to the blueprints on the wall, she added, "I finalized the HVAC contract last night. Their project manager will coordinate with you when they begin work in two days."

"Understood," Drew nodded. "Is there anything else I should know?"

"Nothing significant," Maiya replied. "I've adjusted today's task list based on the volunteers' skills. Since most are unskilled, we'll focus on clearing debris, prepping walls for painting, and setting up scaffolding. Everything is arranged for the major tasks to start once the remediation team finishes their work tonight."

Before Drew could respond, the sound of truck doors slamming outside echoed through the building. Glancing toward the entrance, he saw volunteers emerging from their vehicles—some carrying toolboxes, others with work gloves tucked into their belts. Their voices conveyed a mix of eagerness and apprehension as they approached the building.

Turning back to Maiya, Drew remarked, "Looks like it's time to get started."

She checked her watch and nodded. "Let's make it happen."

LINES IN THE SAND

Drew dusted his hands and glanced at the growing crowd of volunteers. The hum of conversations filled the air, mingling with the crisp scent of sawdust and fresh paint. Some stood in clusters near the folding tables, chatting easily, while others lingered at the edges, holding their tools awkwardly, uncertainty written on their faces.

Beside him, Maiya adjusted her clipboard, giving him a quick look. "We'll start with introductions, then break into teams. You ready?"

Drew nodded. "As ready as I'll ever be."

Maiya stepped forward, raising her voice to carry over the murmurs. "Good morning, everyone! Thank you for being here. Whether this is your first day or you've been with us from the start, you're all an important part of this project."

A few polite nods and scattered smiles met her words. First-day jitters, Drew thought. The mix of energy was familiar—eager hands, hesitant hearts, and the occasional skeptic.

Maiya gestured to him. "For those of you who haven't met him yet, this is Drew, our project manager. He's here to make sure we stay on schedule, keep things safe, and avoid knocking down the wrong walls."

A few chuckles rippled through the group.

Drew gave a small nod, a hint of a smile on his face. "And if you do knock down the wrong wall, just make sure I don't see it."

This time, the laughter was more relaxed, easing some of the tension. Drew caught Maiya's glance—her silent acknowledgment that they had set the right tone.

Then the side door creaked open.

Logan stepped inside, his movements deliberate, shoulders tight. Drew spotted him immediately, noting the hesitation in his step and the guarded look in his eyes. Logan wasn't sure if he belonged here, but he had come anyway. That, Drew thought, was something.

Maiya didn't falter. "And I see we've got some new volunteers today! Welcome, we're glad you're here."

Logan gave a slight nod, his gaze avoiding the crowd as he moved toward the back of the room. Arms crossed, he leaned against the wall, content to keep his distance.

Drew wasn't surprised. He'd seen that restlessness before—the way Logan had lingered in the bookstore, holding the flyer longer than necessary. Logan might not know why he was here yet, but Drew could tell he was searching for something. And showing up was the first step.

The introductions continued smoothly, but just as Maiya was about to wrap up, the door opened again.

Sienna slipped inside.

Her entrance was quieter than Logan's—no stiff shoulders, no hesitation, just a quiet presence that seemed to try not to draw attention. She scanned the room briefly, her fingers brushing the sleeves of her hoodie in a small, almost unconscious gesture of self-comfort.

Some volunteers turned to look. The room's energy shifted, the curiosity in their eyes palpable.

From one of the nearby groups, a voice broke through, low but loud enough to carry. "Well, that's a surprise."

Drew turned toward the source: Elena. Her slight smirk and faux-casual tone made his stomach tighten.

Elena leaned toward the person beside her, her voice laced with thinly veiled judgment. "Didn't think I'd see her here. Guess anyone can volunteer these days."

Drew's jaw tightened. He wasn't the only one who noticed. Sienna had heard.

She didn't flinch. Didn't react. But Drew saw the tension in her shoulders, the way her gaze flickered to the ground for just a moment before steadying. She had expected this.

Drew exhaled slowly. I can plan for blueprints and schedules, but people? That's a whole different kind of challenge. On day one, he didn't want to step on Maiya's authority, but he had a feeling this wouldn't be the last time he'd have to make a call.

Before Drew could step in, another voice rang out.

"That supposed to mean something?" Logan's voice cut through the chatter like a blade.

The room stilled. All eyes shifted toward him. Logan pushed away from the wall, his stance loose, but his tone sharp enough to silence any murmurs.

Elena blinked, clearly caught off guard. "Oh, I didn't mean—"

"Sure, you did," Logan said, his voice calm but unyielding. His gaze locked on hers, steady and unwavering. "You definitely meant it..."

Elena fumbled for words, her confidence faltering under Logan's directness. She cut him off mid-sentence. "I was just surprised, that's all."

Logan tilted his head slightly, his tone softening just enough to disarm her. "Look, it's fine. Just... think about how it sounds next time."

The moment stretched. Volunteers glanced at one another, some looking away awkwardly, others nodding subtly in silent approval. Elena hesitated, her smirk gone. She let out a shallow sigh and turned her attention elsewhere, retreating without another word.

Logan leaned back against the wall, arms crossed. "Well, if that's settled, can we get back to the part where we're actually supposed to be doing something?"

Maiya seized the opportunity. "Good idea," she said smoothly. She stepped forward and gestured toward the project board. "Let's go over today's tasks."

And just like that, the tension dissipated.

As Drew worked to organize the volunteers into teams, he kept an eye on Sienna and Logan.

Sienna hadn't said a word after Elena's comment. She stuck to the edges of the group, her focus sharp but her demeanor guarded. Not withdrawn, Drew noted, but clearly here for the work, not the drama.

Logan, on the other hand, had surprised him. It wasn't just that Logan had spoken up, it was the way he had done it—calm, steady, and with just enough bite to make his point without escalating things. Drew had seen another side of Logan today, one that hinted at a man unwilling to let injustice slide.

Drew caught Sienna glancing at Logan once, briefly. It wasn't gratitude or curiosity, more like recognition, as if she were filing the moment away to process later.

Meanwhile, Maiya passed near Elena, who was walking toward the next task with quieter steps but a voice still low enough to carry. "I just hope she's not here to cause problems," Elena murmured. "We're here to work and accomplish something good. But some people…"

Maiya didn't stop or react, but Drew could tell she'd heard. He saw the faint crease in her brow, the slight tightening of her grip on the clipboard.

"Oh, please don't let her be here to stir things up," Maiya thought, exhaling quietly as she walked over to Drew.

"Well," she said softly, "that was an unexpected contribution from Logan."

Drew smirked. "Yeah. But I'll take it."

Maiya nodded. "Let's keep them busy and see how this plays out. I need to devise a plan to manage this group."

Drew glanced toward Logan and Sienna, who had joined separate teams but still carried the weight of the earlier exchange. "Yeah," he said. "We'll see how it all shakes out."

And with that, they returned to work, the first lines drawn in a group still finding its footing.

FRAMING AND FAULT LINES

The sun was just rising when Drew wheeled Sarah to the community center. The cool morning air carried the scent of damp earth and the quiet promise of progress.

Every morning, ever since Maiya had given him the flyer, Drew and Sarah had made it their routine to pray over the project. Today was no exception. As Drew maneuvered Sarah's wheelchair across the uneven ground, their prayers flowed easily, in rhythm with the soft roll of the wheels.

"Lord, we ask for Your provision," Sarah prayed softly, her voice mingling with the distant traffic. "Provide the skills, tools, and materials we need, right when we need them. Let nothing be delayed."

Drew joined in, his voice steady. "And God, bring peace and unity among the workers. Help us to collaborate, even when challenges arise. Give us wisdom to lead well and reflect Your love in all we do."

The weight of their prayers settled over the site like a quiet blanket. Drew paused for a moment, absorbing it all—the structure of the building, the scattered tools, and the growing hum of volunteers arriving to begin the day. There was still much to do, but each day brought them closer.

As they completed their round and began heading home, the world was fully awake, and another day at the site commenced.

In the afternoon, the community center was bustling with activity. Volunteers hammered, measured, and worked around the site, their energy filling the partially constructed space.

Logan had finished his assigned tasks for the day and checked the project board. Next task: install the utility room door. Mitch glanced over at him. "The kid takes initiative. Maybe he's not a total loser after all," he muttered to himself.

An hour later, Logan knelt by the doorway, feeling increasingly frustrated. The pre-made door frame was square, but the opening was completely off. The settling foundation had thrown the wall out of alignment. He tried to adjust the frame to fit, but every attempt felt futile. The growing gaps and uneven angles mocked his efforts.

Mitch walked past, then stopped, observing Logan struggle.

Logan wasn't making progress, but at least he was persevering. "What are you doing?" Mitch asked sharply, his voice brimming with impatience. Logan straightened up, gripping the frame for support. "Trying to align the frame," he muttered. "The wall's crooked because the foundation settled."

Mitch snorted, moving closer. "So? What, you're just guessing now? That's not the way to go." He pointed at the frame. "You've been at this for a while, and you're making it worse. The frame is square—you maintain that. Use shims to adjust for the wall. Don't just tamper with it like an amateur."

Logan exhaled sharply, his grip on the crowbar tightening. "I was trying to fix it," he snapped.

"Trying?" Mitch's voice grew more exasperated with each word. "You should know how to handle this by now! This isn't a playground, and I'm not here to babysit. If you can't manage something this basic, this isn't the place for you."

The words stung more than they should have, each one a sharp reminder of every time he had been criticized with no guidance on how to improve. Logan hated feeling clueless, judged, dismissed before even getting the chance to explain himself.

Without another word, Logan let the crowbar slip from his hand, the loud clang ringing across the site. He turned and walked away, each angry step echoing in his chest. The pounding matched the frustration that tightened around his ribcage as he headed to a quieter spot behind the building.

Logan paced back and forth, the gravel crunching beneath his boots. His fists clenched and relaxed, the anger bubbling up with each muttered line he rehearsed.

"Mitch, I'm not an idiot," he muttered to himself. "The problem isn't me—it's the wall. Maybe YOU should double-check the work before—" He stopped mid-sentence, shaking his head vigorously. "No, that would only make things worse."

He turned again, boots grinding on the gravel with every step. "Oh, of course, Mitch," he spat sarcastically. "I'll just wave a magic wand and magically align the whole building." He paused, clenching his jaw. "Sure. That will fix everything."

Drew stood a few feet away, leaning against the supply trailer. He didn't interrupt, watching as Logan sighed in frustration and ran a hand through his hair. Drew recognized the look in Logan's eyes—it ran deeper than just frustration. If he didn't intervene now, things might escalate.

When Logan kicked a rock loudly across the gravel, Drew finally spoke.

"Needed to let off some steam?" Drew asked casually.

Logan jumped slightly, turning toward Drew with a sheepish expression. "You heard all of that?"

Drew smirked. "Couldn't miss it. You're pretty vocal when you argue with yourself."

Logan let out a half-laugh, half-sigh. "Yeah, well... it's better than arguing with Mitch."

Drew nodded thoughtfully, his demeanor composed. "Sometimes walking away is the best choice. But it doesn't make it easy."

Logan glanced at him but didn't respond. Drew decided to leave it at that, mentally noting to check in with Logan later.

Inside, Mitch knelt by the doorway, adjusting shims with a grunt. His tape measure clanked against the frame as he worked, muttering under his breath. Maiya approached, clipboard in hand. "How's it going?" she asked, eyeing the doorway.

Mitch didn't look up. "The frame's square, but the wall isn't plumb because the foundation settled," he replied. "Logan was clueless and messed things up."

Maiya nodded calmly. "That's frustrating. I imagine dealing with a crooked wall must be tough without your expertise."

Mitch sighed, sitting back. "I'm used to working with people who know the basics. I've been doing this for years, and sometimes… I forget what it's like to be inexperienced."

Maiya gave him a small, understanding smile. "That's understandable. But Logan's here to learn, and he's doing his best. Can we agree that you were a bit harsh on him?"

Mitch let out a long sigh, rubbing his face. "Yeah. I was. I'll talk to him tomorrow."

Maiya smiled softly. "That's good. He'll appreciate it."

Unbeknownst to Mitch and Maiya, Elena had overheard the confrontation earlier. She had been organizing supplies nearby and caught every word as Mitch criticized Logan. She had seen Logan storm off and heard Mitch's words—'amateurs.'

Elena smiled to herself. Logan had seemed familiar from the moment he arrived to volunteer, and now she understood why. He was the guy from the diner, the one who'd been publicly fired. She'd pieced together the story that day, refilling her coffee, and now she had the gossip she'd been waiting for.

Her eyes gleamed with the juicy tidbits she'd soon share with the right people. Gossip had a way of spreading, especially when it was handled just right.

An older volunteer had also overheard the confrontation with Logan. He approached Mitch, grumbling about the project's history. "Some guy named Keith Ridelson tried this years ago," he said. "But it didn't end well, did it?"

Mitch tightened his grip on the wrench, his jaw clenched. He didn't reply, just focused on his work, though the comment lingered in his mind.

COFFEE ROOM GROUNDING

Rain tapped against the windows of Drew's bookstore, a steady rhythm weaving into the warmth of the coffee nook at the back. At a small table, Drew and Sarah sat hand in hand, their quiet prayer blending with the storm's melody, wrapping the space in a peaceful devotion.

"Lord," Sarah prayed gently, "thank You for this day, even the rain. Let it remind us of Your provision and how You soften even the hardest ground."

"Amen," Drew murmured, his voice steady yet serene. The bell above the door chimed, pulling his attention as Logan stepped inside, rainwater dripping from his hair and soaking through his jacket. He looked weary, his shoulders slightly slumped.

"Storm caught you?" Drew asked with a small smile, gesturing toward the coffee pot.

Logan shrugged off his drenched jacket and hung it on the peg by the door, water pooling beneath it. "Something like that," he muttered, running a hand through his wet hair.

Drew poured a steaming mug of coffee and slid it across the table as Logan sat down. The room filled with the rich aroma of freshly brewed coffee, mingling with the earthy scent of rain-soaked clothes. Logan took a slow sip, exhaling as he set the mug down.

"Mitch was barking orders again yesterday, acting like I should just know what to do. I don't. And no matter how hard I try, it's like he's already decided I'm a screw-up." His jaw tightened, and his voice dropped. "Maybe he's right."

Logan leaned back in his chair, letting out a long, frustrated breath.

Drew nodded thoughtfully, leaning forward slightly. "Logan, taking the time to figure things out doesn't make you a failure. It shows you're trying—and that matters more than getting everything perfect from the start. I'm proud of you for walking away yesterday before things escalated."

Logan let out a slow breath, his fingers tightening around the coffee mug. "Maybe... but it sure feels unsettling."

Drew's smile was warm and reassuring. "You didn't back down —you chose peace. That's no small thing, especially when dealing with someone like Mitch. Honestly, I'm impressed with how you handled it. The way you kept your cool—it's not what the old Logan would've done. You're showing more strength than you realize."

Logan blinked, caught off guard. "You really think so? Because it sure doesn't feel like it."

"It doesn't have to feel like it. You walked away instead of snapping, and that's growth. Let's keep building on that."

Logan ran a hand over the back of his neck, his gaze distant. "I don't know. Mitch just makes it so hard sometimes. I swear, he was trying to make me lose it."

Drew's expression softened. "I know Mitch can be a handful. But have you ever stopped to think about what's behind his attitude?"

Logan frowned, curiosity flickering through his frustration. "What do you mean?"

Drew took a measured sip of his coffee before answering. "Mitch has been doing this kind of work for decades, and he's really good at it. But he's getting older, and he knows he can't manage things the way he used to. That's hard for a guy like him to admit."

He set his mug down, meeting Logan's gaze. "What Mitch really needs is someone he can trust to take on more responsibility—someone who's willing to learn, put in the effort, and step up when it counts. That's you, Logan. You care about doing things right, and that's exactly the kind of attitude Mitch can rely on."

Logan's grip tightened around his coffee mug, his knuckles going white. "I don't know," he muttered, his voice rougher now. "Mitch reminds me too much of my stepfather—always barking orders, acting like nothing's ever good enough. I spent years trying to prove myself to a man who only saw what I did wrong and made sure I never forgot it." His jaw clenched, and he let out a sharp breath through his nose. "I'm not doing that again. I won't."

Drew let the weight of Logan's words settle between them. He didn't rush to fill the silence, didn't try to smooth over the jagged edges. Instead, he nodded slowly.

"I get it," he said, his voice steady. "That kind of hurt doesn't just fade. And I won't pretend Mitch doesn't have his rough edges—he does. But Logan, you're not that kid anymore. You don't have to stand there waiting for someone to knock you down."

Logan's jaw worked, but he stayed silent.

Drew leaned forward slightly, elbows on the table. "Mitch isn't your stepfather. He's got his own way of doing things, and yeah, sometimes that means barking orders. But he's not looking to tear you down. He's looking for someone who can step up." He let the words hang there for a moment, then added, "And maybe—just maybe—this isn't about proving anything to Mitch. It's about proving to yourself that only you get to define you—not your past, not your stepfather, and not Mitch."

Logan exhaled slowly, staring at the dark surface of his coffee. The words made sense—some part of him wanted to believe them —but the past had a way of speaking louder. He could still hear his stepfather's voice, still feel the weight of never being enough.

He clenched his jaw, and the words tumbled out before he could stop them. "And what if you're wrong? What if Mitch really does see me the same way?"

Drew met his gaze without hesitation. "Then don't prove anything to him—prove it to yourself. Show yourself that his voice doesn't get the final say."

Logan's frown deepened. "What if I can't do it? What if I just end up proving Mitch right?"

"You won't," Drew said firmly. "Because you've already shown you're willing to try, and that's more than half the battle. Keep at it, learn what you can, and take it one step at a time. Mitch might never say it aloud, but he'll notice—and that's when you'll realize you're capable of far more than you thought."

GOSSIP AND GRACE

At the community center just a block away, Elena stood near the tool bins, sorting gloves and tape measures into neat piles. The steady patter of rain against the windows provided a quiet backdrop to the buzz of activity inside. Her sharp eyes darted toward the doorway where Mitch had berated Logan the day before. The memory of Mitch's voice still lingered in her mind—loud, cutting, with Logan storming off soon after. Elena smirked to herself. Logan had looked familiar from the moment he'd arrived to volunteer, but it wasn't until yesterday that the memory clicked. He was the guy from the diner—fired in front of everyone. She'd overheard enough that day while refilling her coffee to piece the story together.

"Poor Logan," she murmured under her breath, her tone dripping with mock sympathy. "Seems trouble follows him wherever he goes."

Elena wasn't one to let a good story go to waste. She casually joined a pair of volunteers packing up supplies and leaned in just slightly. "Did you see Logan and Mitch yesterday? That was something, huh?"

One of the volunteers glanced over curiously. "Yeah, I heard some of it. What happened?"

Elena's lips curved into a slow smile. "Oh, you didn't hear?" She lowered her voice just enough to make them lean in. "Turns out I saw him get fired from a diner a few weeks ago. It was... messy."

The other volunteer frowned. "Messy how?"

Elena shrugged slightly, feigning reluctance. "I don't know the full story. But let's just say, it didn't seem like his first time in trouble." She let her words linger, her tone leaving just enough doubt to stir curiosity. Elena's eyes gleamed as she watched the volunteers exchange glances. Satisfied, she watched her little seed of gossip begin to take root.

Elena stood near the tool bins a little while later, her smirk fading into a more neutral expression as she continued sorting supplies. The volunteers she had been chatting with had moved on, and she was left alone with the quiet hum of the community center. Her hands moved methodically as she arranged gloves and tape measures into neat piles, but her thoughts were elsewhere.

The sound of purposeful footsteps echoed across the room, drawing Elena's attention. Almost on cue, Maiya appeared in the doorway, clipboard in hand, her hair damp from the rain outside. She tucked a stray strand behind her ear, her eyes scanning the room with practiced focus.

"Elena," Maiya greeted her warmly, though there was a quiet authority to her voice. "Still working over here?"

Elena glanced up, shifting her expression to one of practiced helpfulness. "Just tidying up a bit," she replied smoothly, gesturing toward the neatly arranged bins. "Trying to keep things organized."

Maiya stepped further into the room, a small smile touching her lips. "I appreciate that. We've got a lot going on today, and it helps to have someone keeping things in order." She tapped the edge of her clipboard with a pen, her focus briefly shifting to her list. "Will you double-check that everything is stocked and lay out what the demo teams will need? Here's a list of the teams and their supplies."

Elena's smile tightened imperceptibly as she took the list from Maiya's hand. "Of course. I'll take care of it."

Maiya nodded, her expression unreadable. "Thanks." She turned to leave, but her thoughts lingered on the trio. Being forced to work together on the wall might push them to confront their issues, especially with Elena. Maiya sighed faintly. *I'll need to see if she can handle this without stirring up more trouble.*

Elena's eyes lingered on Maiya's retreating figure, her expression shifting into something more calculating as she glanced down at the list. Her smirk returned as she scanned the names. "Demo work with Logan and Sienna?" she murmured to herself. "Now that could be interesting."

A quiet chuckle escaped her lips as she set the list aside. *This is going to be fun.*

BREAKING DOWN WALLS

The quiet murmur of conversation surrounded the assignment board as volunteers moved to collect their tasks for the day. Sienna and Logan stood side by side, scanning the list that Maiya had posted. Their names were listed beside a single task: "Demo crumbling wall – south wing."

Logan muttered under his breath, squinting at the board. "Crumbling wall. Sounds like a dream job."

Sienna smirked faintly, folding her arms. "Could be worse."

"Yeah? How?" Logan glanced at her.

"I don't know. Blocked plumbing?" she offered dryly, her lips twitching into a faint grin.

Logan let out a short laugh, shaking his head. "Fair point."

As they headed toward the supply room, Logan's voice softened. "Hey, uh... I owe you an apology."

Sienna slowed her steps, giving him a curious look. "For what?"

"For how I handled things yesterday," he admitted, his voice lower than usual. "I wasn't trying to step on your toes, but I should've thought about how it looked—like I was speaking for you instead of letting you handle it. I've spent too much time assuming people need me to fight their battles."

Sienna tilted her head, her gaze thoughtful. "I didn't take it that way."

"Maybe not," Logan said with a small shrug. "But still, I should've thought it through. You're new here, and I don't really know you... but I've been around enough people like Elena to know how much those comments can sting." He hesitated, meeting her eyes briefly. "I guess I just hate seeing people get talked down to."

Sienna studied him for a moment, her expression unreadable. Then she gave a small nod. "It wasn't great, but I've heard worse," she paused, her voice softening. "Thanks for saying something. You're a thoughtful person."

Logan's lips quirked into a faint smile. "Yeah, well. Let's see how bad this wall is and how easily it'll come down."

When they entered the supply room, both were caught off guard. The tools they needed were already pulled and arranged on a bench: two different-sized sledgehammers, crowbars, heavy gloves, a tarp, and a wheelbarrow.

Elena leaned casually against the workbench, a bright smile stretching across her face—just a little too wide, just a little too smooth, like she was enjoying a private joke. "There you are," she said, her voice dripping with forced cheer. "All set for your big demo work."

Logan exchanged a quick glance with Sienna, who raised an eyebrow but said nothing.

"Thanks," Logan said curtly, his tone neutral, as he walked over to inspect the supplies. He picked up one of the sledgehammers, testing its weight.

"Appreciate it," Sienna added, her voice polite but firm. Then she glanced at the supplies again and frowned slightly. "Are there protective masks? That wall's full of mold."

Elena's smile faltered just slightly before she gestured to a nearby shelf. "Of course. Right there. Didn't think I'd have to get it all out for you."

Sienna gave her a quick glance, walking over to grab two masks and placing them in the wheelbarrow. "Thanks. They are in a new location."

Elena folded her arms, her smirk returning. "No problem."

Logan slipped the mask onto his wrist and turned toward the door. "We've got it covered."

Sienna nodded in quiet agreement, pushing the wheelbarrow toward the hallway. They left the supply room without another word, their strides purposeful.

Once they were out of earshot, Logan exhaled sharply, shaking his head. "Well, that was... something."

Sienna glanced at him, her lips twitching. "She tries."

Logan smirked faintly, adjusting the mask hanging from his wrist. "If you call that trying."

Sienna let out a soft chuckle. "At least the tools are ready. Small victories, right?"

"Yeah," Logan agreed, his tone dry but lighter now. "Let's hope that wall doesn't turn out worse than it looks."

Sienna arched an eyebrow, her voice light with amusement. "What's that? Optimism?"

Logan shrugged, the corner of his mouth lifting in a rare smile. "Always."

The morning sunlight filtered through the cracked windows of the old community center, casting uneven streaks of light across the room. Logan stood in front of the crumbling wall, crowbar in hand. Beside him, Sienna adjusted her gloves, her movements steady and deliberate. She didn't say much—she never really did—but Logan was grateful for the silence. After the chaos of the last few days, the quiet felt almost therapeutic.

He swung the crowbar hard, sending a chunk of plaster to the floor. Dust puffed into the air, catching the sunlight like tiny specks of glitter. Sienna worked alongside him, her motions fluid and controlled, as though the crumbling wall didn't faze her.

Logan muttered under his breath, shaking his head. "This wall's a disaster."

Sienna glanced over, brushing the dust off her gloves. "Yeah," she said softly. "It is."

Logan leaned the crowbar against his shoulder, staring at the exposed beams beneath the plaster. "You think it's worth fixing?"

Sienna paused, tilting her head slightly. "Parts of it are," she said. "The rest... we clear out and start fresh."

They worked in silence after that, the sound of their tools filling the space. Sienna didn't try to make conversation, didn't try to analyze him. She just stayed beside him, steady and patient, letting the moment be what it was.

Logan pried at a warped wooden stud, his movements sharp and forceful. Beneath the layers of damage, something surprising emerged.

"Hey, look at this," he said, motioning to Sienna. "The outside's shot, but the studs are solid. It just needs some reinforcement."

Sienna stepped closer, brushing dust from her gloves. "Guess it's like anything else," she said. "Not everything has to be thrown out. You just fix what's broken and keep what's still strong."

Logan leaned against the crowbar, staring at the exposed framework of the wall. Something about her words stuck with him, unsettling and sharp.

He thought about the fights he'd had over the years, the jobs lost, the people pushed away. He had spent his whole life blaming others for his anger and frustration, his stepdad, his coworkers, anyone who didn't 'measure up.'

But this wall didn't fall apart overnight. It had weakened bit by bit, layer after layer, until all it took was one hard hit to make it collapse. It wasn't weak. It was neglected. Just like him.

Logan exhaled slowly, gripping the crowbar a little tighter. "Not everything has to be thrown out," he murmured under his breath.

Sienna glanced at him. "What was that?"

Logan shook his head. "Nothing." He turned back to the framework, his next swing slower, more deliberate.

Sienna didn't push him to speak again. She just kept working beside him, meeting him exactly where he was—dusty, guarded, and broken, but still standing.

At the end of the workday, Logan and Sienna swept up the debris in silence. The floor was littered with plaster dust and broken pieces of wood, but the wall frame stood steady and exposed, ready for the next steps.

As they finished, Logan surprised himself.

"Hey, uh… thanks," he muttered, shifting awkwardly.

Sienna looked up, her expression cautious but curious. "For what?"

"For not making this harder than it had to be," Logan said, rubbing the back of his neck. "You didn't ask questions or try to fix anything. You just… let me figure it out."

Sienna's lips quirked into a faint smile. "Guess I'm not much for idle chatter."

Logan chuckled softly, his gaze briefly meeting hers. "Good. I think I've had enough of those."

As they gathered the last of the tools, Logan exhaled, feeling something lighter settle in his chest. The wall was gone. Not just the one in front of him—but the one he'd been carrying for years.

A HUG THAT HEALS

Sienna sat curled in the old wooden rocker, its creak the only sound in her tiny apartment. The rocker had once belonged to Granny—shipped across states and years to land in this quiet corner by the window. A chipped teacup sat in her hands, filled with chamomile mint tea. The steam rose in lazy spirals, the scent wrapping around her like a memory she hadn't meant to revisit.

Some memories don't fade. They stay sharp and alive, like a movie playing on a loop behind your eyes. For Sienna, this one always began the same way: the creak of the porch boards beneath her feet, the chipped teacup, the golden light stretching across the yard.

She could almost feel it—like she was there again.

Sienna paced the porch, her bare feet brushing against the old wooden boards, each step punctuated by the creaks beneath her. She was bracing for a conversation she'd put off for far too long.

The scent of chamomile and mint floated from the teacup sitting untouched on the small side table. But Sienna couldn't sit, couldn't settle into the warmth of a place that had once felt safe. Not with the storm inside her.

She folded her arms tightly across her chest, exhaling sharply. "I don't even know where to start." Her voice was tight, like she was barely holding together.

Granny sat in her old rocking chair, hands resting gently in her lap. She didn't rush, didn't push. Just rocked, slow and steady, her eyes soft, waiting.

Sienna's voice cracked. "You'll hate me when I tell you."

The chair creaked as Granny rocked, unfazed. "I don't think that's true, baby girl," she said, steady as ever.

Sienna turned sharply. The words tumbled out before she could stop them. "You don't know, Granny. You don't know how hard it's been—how much I've had to do just to keep going."

She dug her fingers into her arms, gripping herself like she was bracing for impact. Granny didn't flinch. Didn't react with shock. Just waited.

Sienna pressed the heels of her hands against her eyes. She'd spent so long holding everything in, it felt unnatural to let it out.

Her breath shuddered as she spoke again, her voice trembling. "I left home, Granny. I ran because I couldn't—because I was drowning. I was sixteen and pregnant, and I thought if I told them, they'd never look at me the same. I didn't even get to choose how it happened—it just... happened."

She paused, a hollow laugh escaping her. "I thought leaving was my only way out. My parents wouldn't have taken my word against his, so I left. I couldn't bear the thought of enduring judgment for something that was forced on me. But when I lost the baby... I realized that pain was just as deep, just as real."

She drew in an unsteady breath. "I stayed away. Got my GED. Worked two jobs. Took night classes. Even earned an associate's degree—thought that would open doors. But the best I could get was a night data entry job. It's not glamorous, but it keeps the lights on. I kept telling myself if I could just do everything right, maybe I'd stop feeling so wrong inside."

"I was alone. No family. No help. Just... me." She gave a bitter, hollow laugh. "And you'd think I'd have figured it out by now, but

I haven't. Every day, I wake up like I'm barely keeping my head above water."

Her voice dropped, almost too soft to hear. "The pills make it easier. Or at least they used to. A coworker gave me one on a rough day—said they weren't addictive. I knew better, but I was so tired. Tired of pretending I was okay. So I said yes. And then I kept saying yes."

Silence settled between them. Then, the soft creak of the rocking chair sounded, and Granny stood. Sienna didn't move. Didn't turn around. She braced herself for judgment, for disappointment.

But instead, a warm hand brushed away a tear. Granny's voice was soft, no anger, no shame—just love. "I am so sorry, my dear sweet Sienna."

Sienna turned slowly, blinking through the blur of her tears. She looked into Granny's eyes and saw no condemnation, only love. No judgment. Just love.

"I hear you," Granny said, her voice thick with emotion. "I see your pain. And I love you so much. Thank you for having the courage to share that with me."

The floodgates broke open. Sienna's legs gave out, and Granny caught her, holding her tightly like she never intended to let go. Sienna sobbed—hard, gut-wrenching sobs that shook her entire body. But it wasn't just pain spilling out. It was relief. Relief at being seen. At being heard. At being loved for who she was—not for what she thought she should be.

Granny just held her, steady and strong, rocking her gently as she had when Sienna was little.

When the sobs finally slowed, Granny stepped back just enough to meet Sienna's tear-streaked gaze. She rested her hands on Sienna's shoulders, firm but gentle. Sienna let out a shaky breath.

For the first time in forever, she wasn't carrying it alone.

That moment on the porch burned itself into Sienna's memory, like sunlight fading an old photograph. It was the first time she had ever let herself be fully seen—no walls, no masks, no pretending. And Granny's love hadn't wavered.

It didn't fix everything. Healing didn't come overnight. The road ahead was still long, messy, and filled with battles she hadn't yet fought. But that hug was the first step. The moment she started to believe—just a little—that maybe, just maybe, she didn't have to carry it all alone.

She blinked slowly, returning to the present: her tiny apartment, the familiar creak of Granny's rocker, and the warmth of the cup in her hands. The memory still lingered, soft around the edges.

She glanced down at the chamomile mint tea in her cup. A faint smile tugged at her lips. This time, she drank it. Slowly. Like it was safe now. Like it was hers to savor.

She could almost hear Granny's voice. "It's never too late to start over."

It was Granny who gave her a name—a woman who ran a small rehab with a Bible in her bag and stories in her eyes. That's where the real rebuilding started. Not with the pills. Not with the pain. But with the truth.

CRACKS BENEATH
THE SURFACE

Elena wasn't one for attachments. She'd learned that lesson long ago—people didn't stay, plans didn't work, and no matter how much you desired smoothness, something always went awry. That was just life. Yet, for reasons she couldn't explain, she kept returning here.

The community center smelled of sawdust and fresh paint, a sharp contrast to the stale air of her apartment. It was noisy, chaotic, and filled with people who genuinely believed in their actions. It unsettled her. She didn't oppose volunteering. She simply didn't engage in 'causes.' She engaged in projects. Projects had clear beginnings and endings. They didn't demand personal involvement—just effort. You invested in work, tasks were completed, and you moved on. Simple. This? This was not a project. This involved people. And people were always intriguing —if only because they provided something to dissect, something to scrutinize until their imperfections emerged.

Elena entered the storage room, her heels clicking softly on the concrete floor as she surveyed the disorder. Stacks of lumber leaned against the walls, partially used paint cans lined the shelves, and tools lay scattered in between. In the center stood Logan, arms folded, glaring at a pile of boards as if expecting them to apologize. "Of course," she muttered, "Why would it be organized?" Leaning against the doorway, she spoke with a hint of amusement, "Are you waiting for them to move by themselves?"

Logan turned slightly, his expression unreadable. "No. Just figuring out where to begin."

"Not your strong suit?" she teased.

He didn't take the bait, though his eyes narrowed slightly, more inquisitive than irritated. "Are you always this helpful?"

"Only when I see someone struggling," Elena replied, folding her arms as if critiquing his approach was her sole purpose.

Logan chuckled, grabbed a board, and shifted it needlessly, just to stay busy. "Let me guess—you're one of those 'everything in its place' people, aren't you?"

Elena shrugged, implying the answer was obvious. "Organization enhances efficiency. You'd be surprised how things improve when you don't just toss everything in a pile and hope for the best."

Tapping a stack, Logan's faint smirk held a teasing quality. "Funny thing about piles. Sometimes they topple, and sometimes..." He shrugged casually, meeting her gaze with a dry humor glint. "They just stay put."

Caught off guard by his unexpected response, Elena considered him for a moment. Maybe he wasn't as predictable as she thought. Without a word, she fetched a clipboard from a shelf and explained, "We'll sort by size first, then by material. Otherwise, you'll waste time searching for what you need."

Though sighing, Logan grabbed another board and began moving it, reluctantly following her lead. "Fine. But if you start using color-coded labels, I'm out."

Suppressing a laugh, Elena nodded. "Noted." Tension momentarily eased between them, resembling teamwork. "You know," Elena remarked later, her tone lighter, "this would be quicker if you didn't handle one board at a time."

Raising an eyebrow, Logan focused on his task. "And this would be faster if you actually helped instead of supervising."

Chuckling, Elena stacked a few planks neatly. "Fair enough." They worked in silence, but Elena kept her guard up, her gaze scanning the room. "Well, I'll leave you to it. I'm sure you have it under control now."

"Sure. Thanks for the help," Logan replied, his attention on the task.

As Elena turned to leave, Logan exhaled softly, anticipating her return. A faint smile tugged at the corner of his mouth as he resumed working.

An hour later, the disorder had transformed into a system. With Logan reassigned to another project, Elena was finishing her tasks when Maiya checked on the progress. The warmth in her smile made Elena uncomfortable, as if she had been seen through, and she wasn't sure whether that made her want to retreat further or lean in.

"You're skilled at keeping things in order," Maiya complimented.

Elena wiped a stray strand of hair from her eyes. "It's just organizing."

Maiya's gaze softened, as if she could see more than just the task at hand. "It's more than that. You identify what needs to be done and do it. Not everyone possesses that skill."

Uncomfortable with the praise, Elena downplayed it. "Just common sense."

Maiya's tone remained light but sincere. "Still, if you ever consider helping with planning, we could use someone like you."

The invitation unsettled Elena, as if it was more than just an offer—it was a challenge to step into something she didn't know how to handle. "I'm not really into long-term commitments."

Maiya smiled knowingly, but there was no insistence in her voice. "Of course." Yet the open-endedness of the offer lingered, making Elena feel exposed in a way she wasn't used to.

That evening, as Elena packed up, she found herself watching Logan converse quietly with Drew. Logan had been publicly dismissed from his prior job, and those events held meaning. They indicated something. Elena had waited for signs of imperfection —short temper, recklessness, the inevitable mistake—but found none. Logan avoided conflicts, remained composed. He defied her expectations.

She paused. Perhaps she hadn't scrutinized closely enough. People, she believed, didn't change. They just became adept at hiding their true selves. And she excelled at uncovering those facades. But Logan... Logan was different. He had yet to reveal his cracks.

KEITH'S FIRST VISIT

The community center had transformed into more than just a construction site — it had become a space where walls, both physical and emotional, were being dismantled. Logan had sensed this earlier in the day when he finally expressed his thoughts, and Maiya felt it now as she stood next to Drew, assessing the progress that had been made. The ramp was nearing completion, the building's structure was solid, and the volunteers worked with a clear sense of purpose. However, when Keith Ridelson appeared at the periphery of the property, hands tucked into his jacket pockets, Maiya's attention became laser-focused. His presence was unexpected, though not entirely surprising. She hadn't forgotten his pointed remarks during the planning meeting; blunt and dismissive, they had stung deeply but had also lit a fire in her. Now, as he approached, she steadied herself, determined to remain composed.

"Mr. Ridelson," she greeted him, her voice steady yet measured. Drew, standing alongside her with a clipboard, turned to see Keith approaching. Coming to a stop a few steps away, Keith scanned the site, his expression unreadable.

Mitch stood near the back, arms crossed, his gaze locked on Keith. He said nothing, but the weight in his stance made it clear he wasn't just here to observe.

Keith's gaze settled on Mitch for a fraction of a second, a flicker of recognition passing through his eyes before he turned back to Maiya. A charged silence stretched between them — one that spoke of something unfinished. Then, just as quickly, Mitch looked away.

"I didn't expect to see you here," Maiya continued, taking a step toward him. She gestured toward Drew, who stepped forward. "This is Drew, my second-in-command." Drew shook Keith's hand, his smile warm and welcoming. "A pleasure to meet you, Mr. Ridelson." Keith shook Drew's hand firmly, a faint smile appearing on his lips.

"Just Keith, please. No need for formalities." Keith's demeanor seemed different from the planning meeting.

Though his earlier remarks had weighed on her for days, now he appeared more measured, more observant. "What brings you by today?" she inquired, maintaining a cordial tone.

Keith's gaze moved over the volunteers, the partially completed ramp, and the framework of the building. Pausing slightly at the doorway, his eyes seemed to settle on something only he could see before returning to Maiya. "I wanted to see how things were progressing," he stated simply. "You've made significant strides with this place. It's really coming together."

Maiya allowed herself a small smile, pride evident in her voice. "We've received tremendous support. The community has been amazing." Keith nodded, his gaze once again drifting toward the building. An expression that hinted at nostalgia or regret briefly crossed his face before vanishing. "I can tell that this project means a lot to you," he remarked quietly. "That's commendable to see."

"It does," Maiya affirmed. "This place has always held significance for the community. It deserves to be reconstructed."

Keith studied her for a moment, his expression contemplative. "That's good to hear," he finally said, though his tone became slightly more pointed. "Passion alone doesn't complete a project. Precision is key. Without attention to detail, even the best intentions can unravel."

Her smile wavered as his words reminded her of the planning meeting. The sting had faded over time, replaced by determination — but it wasn't entirely gone. There was truth in what he was saying; there always was, but that didn't make it easier to hear. "We are striving to maintain a balance," she replied evenly. "It's challenging, but we're navigating through it."

Drew interjected with a light chuckle, offering his reassurance. "Her dedication surpasses that of anyone I've worked with. We are in capable hands, believe me."

Keith's faint smile returned, though it did not reach his eyes entirely. "Determination is crucial," he remarked, "but don't let it cloud your judgment. And remember to adhere to the regulations. They are less forgiving than people realize." Keith's attention drifted to the ramp, his gaze lingering a little longer than necessary. His fingers tapped against the railing, deliberate and expectant.

After a moment, he finally asked, "Who designed this?"

Maiya stepped beside him, keeping her voice steady. "We based it on ADA guidelines. The slope is within the specified range."

Drew nodded. "I personally verified it. It meets the requirements."

Keith gave a slow nod, the kind that wasn't quite agreement, just acknowledgment.

"It meets the previous requirements," he said at last. "Before the code revision earlier this year."

Maiya's brow furrowed. She hadn't caught that. "The slope meets the requirements," she pointed out.

"It does," Keith agreed, his gaze still on the landing. "But the new update changed the required deck size at the base and at each landing. The extra clearance is meant to accommodate newer accessibility standards, especially for turns and transitions."

Drew stiffened slightly, his expression unreadable. "I reviewed the guidelines," he said. "I don't remember seeing anything that would require that adjustment."

Keith finally turned to face him. "Because it wasn't a widely publicized update, and technically may not apply if your inspection occurs before the effective date," he explained. "It will be close. That's why so many builds in progress are going to fail their inspections this year." His fingers brushed the railing once before he stepped back.

"It's a solid build," he admitted. "You did it right — by last year's standards. But you'll want to get ahead of this before it costs you."

Maiya exhaled, already mentally calculating how much effort the change would take. "I wasn't aware of the revision," she admitted. "Thanks for pointing it out."

Keith simply nodded.

After Keith headed out, Drew and Maiya assessed the conversation. He hadn't come to embarrass them, just to see if they'd caught what others might have missed.

No sooner had Keith stepped away from them than a voice called out, "Oh, Maiya!" It was Elena. Her tone was light but laced with false sweetness. "Do you know who that was?"

Maiya stopped mid-step, her shoulders tightening as she slowly turned. Drew, already sensing trouble, remained quiet. Elena crossed her arms, leaning casually against the doorway. "Keith Ridelson. He's the one who abandoned this place years ago. Ran out of money, walked away like it wasn't his problem, and the city had to clean up the mess. Now he's here, acting like he cares? Honestly, I don't know how you can stand it."

Drew frowned, his voice calm but firm. "That's a pretty serious claim, Elena."

"Well, it's true," she said with a dramatic shrug. "Ask anyone. He's always looking for a way to make himself look good." Unbeknownst to them, Keith had stopped just outside the doorway, his hand resting on the frame. Her words hit him like a slap — sharp and deliberate. His jaw tightened, and for a moment, he considered stepping back inside to confront her. But he hesitated. People like her didn't care about the truth — they cared about the drama. Keith let out a slow breath and stepped away, his hand gripping the truck keys in his pocket. As he walked, the words replayed in his head, loud and unrelenting. *Quitter. Pretending to care. Walking away.* Sliding into the driver's seat, Keith gripped the steering wheel tightly, his knuckles white. He started the engine, the low rumble filling the cab, but his gaze lingered on the site in the rearview mirror. For a moment, he sat frozen, the weight of the past pressing against his chest like a stone.

CLEARING THE AIR

The quiet coffee room at the back of the bookstore was filled with the soft scratch of Sarah's pen against paper as she sat at one of the small tables, surrounded by a neat stack of invoices and receipts. The room carried a faint smell of fresh coffee, mixed with the lingering scent of books from the main store. When the door creaked open, Sarah looked up to see Maiya and Drew enter. Maiya appeared tense, arms crossed tightly over her chest, while Drew followed behind with a calm and thoughtful expression.

Setting her pen down, Sarah arched an eyebrow and asked, "What's going on? You both look like you've had quite a morning."

Maiya muttered something under her breath, took a seat, and leaned forward, pressing her hands to her temples. Drew sat beside her, giving her a moment to compose herself.

"Elena happened," Drew explained simply. "She dropped one of her classic half-truths — this time about Keith Ridelson."

"Curious," Sarah said, intrigued. "Keith Ridelson? Who's that?"

Maiya sighed. "He's the guy who showed up at the site today, pointing out issues with the project. The same guy who questioned my qualifications during a previous meeting."

Surprised, Sarah asked, "And now he's showing interest in the center again?"

"I guess so," Maiya replied. "It's hard to separate emotions from the facts."

Sarah's gaze softened. "It's hard because you care. And that's a good thing, Maiya. But caring also means being willing to hear the full story — even if it's not what you expected."

Drew nodded. "Exactly. If there's more to his side, don't you think we should investigate it?"

Maiya exhaled slowly, her frustration giving way to uncertainty. "I don't know if I'm ready for that."

Drew considered this, then reached for his phone. "The sooner we get to the truth, the better."

Maiya blinked at him, startled. "Now?"

"Why not?" Drew asked. "If we let rumors fester, they'll only get worse. If he has nothing to hide, he'll be willing to talk."

Sarah nodded. "And if he's serious about wanting to help, this is his chance to prove it."

Maiya hesitated, then let out a slow breath. "Fine. Call him."

Drew dialed. Keith answered after two rings, his voice cautious. Drew mentioned having questions after their earlier conversation. Keith said he was still in the area if they wanted to talk now.

"Great. Can you come to Olive Street Books & Coffee?" Drew asked. "It's just a block from the site."

Keith didn't hesitate. "I know where it is. I'll be there in ten minutes."

Drew glanced at Maiya, who gave a small, reluctant nod. "Sounds good. See you soon."

Keith grabbed the worn folder from the passenger seat — the same one that had once held his plans for the community center. The papers inside were frayed from years of storage, but the details still mattered.

Stepping out of the truck, he took a steady breath, his grip tightening on the edges of the folder. The past couldn't be rewritten. But maybe — just maybe — it wasn't too late to add something new.

As he entered the coffee room, he glanced briefly at Sarah, then Drew, before finally settling on Maiya.

"Before I answer your questions, may I say something?" he asked, his voice steady but reserved.

"Sure," Drew replied, curious.

Maiya straightened in her chair, emotions churning — confusion, frustration, and something else she couldn't quite name. She looked at Keith but didn't speak.

Keith, unfazed by the silence, took a slow step forward. "First, I wanted to apologize," he said, his voice sincere. His gaze rested on Maiya. "I was too harsh at the planning meeting. I had my doubts about whether the project could be completed. But that doesn't excuse the way I dismissed your leadership. You've done great work. What you and Drew have accomplished is impressive. Really impressive."

Maiya blinked, caught off guard by the unexpected compliment. She didn't know whether to feel relieved, validated, or suspicious of his intentions. Her fingers fidgeted slightly with the edge of the table as she processed his words.

Drew, sitting beside her, nodded once but said nothing, waiting to see where Keith would go next.

Keith cleared his throat. "Also," he began carefully, "I overheard someone as I was leaving today, and before it gets out of control, I should set the facts straight."

He hesitated, his grip tightening on the folder. "I worked on the center before, back when the project was still in its early phases. Mitch was one of the tradesmen brought in at the time — he probably never mentioned it, did he?"

Maiya blinked, her grip tightening on the table. "Mitch?"

Keith sighed and shook his head slightly. "Didn't think so. He wasn't around for long — just worked on a few parts of the structure before things fell apart. But he knew how much this place meant to me."

He took a breath, then continued. "What forced me to walk away had nothing to do with the center itself."

Maiya frowned. "Then what happened?"

"When I left, rumors had already started — some partially true, others not. But the truth is, I didn't leave because I didn't care. Early in the project, a competitor tried to force me out of business. He filed a lawsuit related to another project. The case dragged on for years, draining everything — money, resources, my reputation. In the end, I had no choice but to turn the center back over to the city while the legal battle ran its course. I knew the rumors were spreading, but I couldn't risk dragging the project down with me. So, instead of holding on, I pushed for the city to find another buyer."

He placed the folder on the table and opened it, revealing a stack of frayed newspaper clippings and documents.

"This one explains what happened and shows that I won the lawsuit and have finally been awarded damages. And this one—" he pointed to another, "—documents the efforts I made to bring the project back. I never stopped pushing for the city to revisit it. Unfortunately, with changes in administration and the financial market, it took far too long."

Maiya stared at the articles, her throat tightening. She reached out, hesitating before her fingers brushed the edge of the paper. Her hesitation didn't vanish, but it wavered, unsettled by the weight of what she was seeing.

Keith spoke again. "I know how it might look — showing up after all these years, especially with everything that's happened. I thought it was important to clarify my role before assumptions solidified."

Maiya took a deep breath and exhaled slowly. "Why didn't you say any of this earlier?" Her voice was quieter now, but not without edge.

Keith met her gaze, earnest but guarded. "Because this was never about me," he said simply. "It's about the center. About making sure it finally gets finished."

Drew nodded, his voice sincere. "Keith, thank you for sharing this. It means a lot."

Keith nodded, but his eyes remained on Maiya. "I don't expect you to trust me right away. But I meant what I said — I want to see this through. Whether you let me be part of it or not, I'll do whatever I can to make sure this place succeeds."

He glanced between them. "You said you had questions. Have I answered them?"

Drew looked to Maiya. She hesitated, then said softly, "Honestly? You just answered more than we knew to ask."

Keith exhaled, tapping the folder lightly. "I know trust isn't given overnight. I just wanted you to have the truth."

He didn't move to leave immediately. "Take your time going through it. If you have more questions later, I won't be hard to find. Thanks for hearing me out."

With that, he left.

As the door shut behind him, Maiya stared at the articles spread across the table. For a long moment, no one spoke.

"I still don't know how I feel about all this," Maiya admitted. "But I can at least admit I didn't have the full picture before."

Sarah glanced at Drew, then back at Maiya. "That's understandable," she said gently.

The facts were in front of her — but did they change anything?

Drew's voice was quiet. "So... what are you thinking?"

Maiya let out a breath, eyes fixed on the documents in front of her. "I don't know yet. But I do know one thing — I need to see for myself."

THE WEIGHT
OF WORDS

The community center was taking shape — not just patched walls and fresh paint, but something substantial. A meaningful place that could truly make a difference.

The atmosphere had evolved over the past few weeks. There was less demolition now, fewer power tools screeching through unfinished spaces. Instead, there were conversations — people joking, planning, finalizing details. The hardest part was over, at least physically.

Sienna adjusted her grip on a stack of trim boards, careful not to let them shift as she carried them toward the main workspace.

Then she heard it.

Elena.

She wasn't facing Sienna — her back turned as she chatted with another volunteer near the supply table.

"I still can't believe they let Sienna work here. I mean, sure, she's been helping, but rehab? You never really know, do you?"

Sienna's chest tightened, but this time something different flared beneath the familiar sting.

Frustration.

It wasn't the first time Elena had said something like this.

It wouldn't be the last.

Sienna's fingers twitched against the wood. Her feet hesitated for half a second — not much, but enough to feel the battle waging inside her.

The words were right there, just waiting to come out.

But what would they change? Would they stop Elena from talking? Would they silence the whispers that came next — and the ones after that?

Probably not.

One day — one day soon — Sienna wouldn't just walk past.

But not today.

She straightened her shoulders, lifted her chin, and walked right past Elena without so much as a glance. She reached her work area and set the trim boards down with more force than necessary.

The sting of Elena's words sat heavy in her chest. It shouldn't have mattered. She wasn't that person anymore.

Three years. That's how long she had been clean. Three years of fighting for normalcy, for a second chance.

People like Elena only ever saw the mistakes — never the fight.

Sienna inhaled slowly, forcing her shoulders to relax, pushing through the pain and frustration of repeatedly having to carry her past like a shadow. She was more than her worst moment. But that didn't mean she got to erase it.

"You good?" Logan's voice pulled her back.

He was cutting a piece of window trim, giving her a quick glance before adjusting the wood on the saw.

Sienna exhaled, easing her tense grip on the hammer. "Just the local gossip at it again."

Logan studied her, then let out a breath. "Yeah. She seems to be getting worse."

Something about the way he said it made her pause. It wasn't flippant. Not dismissive.

She leaned against the unfinished wall, arms crossed. "You've changed."

Logan smirked, lining up the saw. "Don't tell anyone."

But Sienna didn't let it go. She nodded toward him. "No, really. I noticed it. You don't snap as much. You don't let things get to you like you used to."

Logan didn't answer right away. He just steadied the trim piece and made a clean cut.

"I've been talking to Drew," he admitted.

Sienna raised an eyebrow. "Drew?"

"Yeah. We talk sometimes. He helps me see things differently." He rubbed the back of his neck, glancing down at the wood in his hands. "He doesn't tell me what to do. Just... listens. Asks the right questions. He makes me realize when I'm about to do something stupid — before I do it."

Sienna studied him. Logan had changed. The sharp edges were still there, but they weren't as jagged. He didn't bite back immediately anymore. Didn't bristle at everything.

She hesitated. The words were out before she could stop them. "I wish I had that."

Logan glanced at her, then said, "His wife, Sarah — she's like that too. She listens."

Sienna hesitated again. She didn't know much about Sarah. They'd never had a real conversation, but something about her had always seemed... steady. People were comfortable around her. And Drew spoke about her with a kind of quiet respect that made Sienna wonder.

Since her Granny's death, she hadn't had anyone who truly listened. Not just heard her words, but **listened.**

Sienna swallowed hard.

She had spent so long guarding herself, making sure no one saw the cracks.

What if... she didn't have to?

She didn't know Sarah. Not really.

But maybe — just maybe — that was the point.

She exhaled, running her hand over the edge of the trim board, feeling the smoothness beneath her fingers. The thought lingered.

And for the first time in years, she wasn't sure she wanted it to fade.

A PLACE TO LAND

Sienna paused outside the bookstore, uncertain if she was ready to talk to anyone. She reminded herself she was in control. *It's just coffee. Nothing more.*

That's what she told herself, anyway. But even as she stepped inside, her stomach twisted—not with hunger, but with something she couldn't quite name. Coffee was just an excuse. She could've grabbed a cup anywhere.

But she didn't.

She came *here*.

And that meant something.

She stepped inside, blinking as her eyes adjusted from the bright morning light to the cozy dimness. The familiar scent of coffee and old books filled the air, grounding her for just a moment. She hadn't planned to stop by, but after leaving work, exhaustion had settled deep in her bones. The thought of heading home to an empty apartment without coffee—and already running late—had nudged her through the door.

Behind the counter, Sarah hummed quietly as she sorted a stack of papers. Sienna hesitated. They had only met once, briefly, when Sarah and Drew stopped by the community center. But Logan had mentioned that Sarah was easy to talk to—that she *listened*.

Sarah looked up and offered a warm smile. "Sienna, right? We met a few months ago at the center."

Sienna nodded. "Yeah. Hey... I heard there's coffee here." She shifted slightly, uncomfortable with how awkward that sounded. "I didn't have time to make any before work and figured I'd stop in."

Sarah set down her pen. "You heard right. There's always coffee here." She gestured toward the small coffee station. "Want it to go, or do you have time to sit for a bit?"

Sienna hesitated. Sitting felt like an invitation to talk, and she wasn't quite ready for that. But taking it to go meant leaving right away, and for some reason, she wasn't ready for that either.

"To go, please. I need to get to the community center," she said finally.

Sarah nodded and moved toward the coffee station, still humming as she poured. The sound was soothing, effortless—like someone completely at ease in her space. Sienna found herself watching, studying the way Sarah moved with quiet confidence. She didn't rush. She didn't fill the silence with unnecessary words. She just let things *be*.

That was different. Most people tried too hard and talked too much. But Sarah? She understood the value of quiet.

As she waited, Sienna's eyes drifted to a small stack of bookmarks on the counter—deep blue with gold lettering that read *Olive Street Books & Coffee*, along with the store hours. Without thinking, she picked one up, running her thumb along the edge, feeling the texture of the faux leather. It was sturdy—the kind of thing you kept rather than tossed. Her Granny had always tucked bookmarks into her Bible, slips of paper worn soft from years of use.

Sienna didn't read much these days. But for some reason, she didn't put this one back.

Sarah handed her the cup. "Here you go."

Sienna re-secured the lid, then wrapped her hands around the warmth of the cup, glancing toward the door. "This place... you and Drew run it?"

Sarah nodded. "Initially, Drew managed it, but now I do since he's involved with the community center."

Sienna took a sip, letting the warmth settle inside her. "It's a nice place," she said after a moment. "I can see why people like it."

Sarah smiled. "We like it, too. It's a good fit."

Sienna nodded, shifting the cup in her hands. "Thanks," she said finally. "For the coffee. It's perfect."

"Anytime," Sarah replied. "Stop by whenever you'd like—coffee's always free."

Sienna hesitated, then slipped the bookmark into her pocket before heading for the door. She didn't look back, but somehow, she knew Sarah was still there.

As she stepped outside, she exhaled slowly. She hadn't realized how much she needed that brief moment of stillness—of being *seen* without expectation.

The street felt a little quieter as she walked. She took another sip, fingers absently tracing the edge of the bookmark in her pocket.

Maybe she would stop by again.

She wasn't sure what it meant—that she even considered coming back—but she let the thought settle as she sipped her coffee.

And for the first time in a long time, the idea of coming back didn't feel so impossible.

Unplanned visits became a pattern. Something about the bookstore kept beckoning her. Maybe it was the way Sarah never pried, never asked too much. Or maybe it was something quieter in her kindness—something that reminded Sienna of Granny.

Regardless of the reason, she found herself returning. First just for coffee. Then lingering by the bookshelves. Eventually, sitting in the corner with a book she barely read.

Sarah never questioned it.

She never pushed, never looked at her with pity.

Somehow, she always knew when to leave Sienna alone—and when to slide a second cup of coffee across the table.

Today was Sienna's first full day off in weeks. She could've used it to catch up on rest or tackle her never-ending to-do list. Instead, she found herself here again.

Upon entering the bookstore, she tried to convince herself it was solely for coffee.

It always boiled down to *just coffee*.

But deep down, she knew that wasn't entirely true.

The scent of fresh coffee and worn pages wrapped around her, grounding her in a way she hadn't expected. A space that didn't demand anything. A space that wasn't empty—but wasn't overwhelming either.

She didn't know what she was looking for. Maybe just a quiet moment. A place to breathe. Or maybe something to drown out the noise in her head.

It had been days since she overheard Elena's latest comment. Nothing she hadn't said before—just another version of the same old story. Sienna hadn't even stopped walking when she heard it. The tone was casual, cutting—like she wasn't even a person. Just a whispered warning. A reminder that some people would always see her as a risk, a question mark, a mistake waiting to happen.

Sienna kept moving. Pretended it didn't touch her.

But the words had followed her anyway, curling around her ribs like smoke she couldn't clear.

She had fought so hard to put that part of her life behind her. Yet somehow, it always found a way back. Elena's words refused to let go—like an infected wound that just wouldn't heal.

Sienna ran her fingers along the spines of the books near the back wall, not really reading the titles—just letting the weight of them settle something inside her.

It didn't work.

This was stupid.

She should just go.

"Sienna? Hi! It's so nice to see you!"

She stiffened.

She already knew who it was before she turned.

Sarah sat behind the counter, hands resting lightly on the surface, her expression warm—like she'd been expecting her all along.

"Coffee's brewing if you'd like a cup," Sarah said easily, as if it was the simplest thing in the world.

Sienna hesitated for a fraction of a second too long.

That was all it took for Sarah to see through her.

But she didn't call her out on it. She just poured two cups and slid one across the counter.

"Come on in and make yourself comfortable. I'll be back in a minute."

Sienna could have walked out the door.

She *should* have.

But something in Sarah's easy kindness—the way she poured that second cup without hesitation—settled the part of her that had been unraveling all morning.

The fight to leave dissipated.

Instead, she let herself stay.

LOGAN STEPS IN

Sienna focused on steadying her brushstrokes, moving the roller in smooth, even motions across the drywall. The muted hum of conversation filled the community center—volunteers moving between tasks. For the first time in a long time, the atmosphere felt lighter. Like progress was being made—not just on the walls, but in the people working side by side.

Then she heard it.

Elena's voice was light, almost casual, as if she weren't talking about a real person. "I still can't believe they let Sienna work here. I mean, sure, she's been helping, but rehab? You never really know, do you?"

The words landed like a cold slap. Sharp. Dismissive. A whispered warning meant to linger. A reminder that some people would always see her as a risk. A question mark. A mistake waiting to happen.

Sienna kept painting, pretending it didn't touch her.

But the words wrapped around her ribs like smoke she couldn't clear. Her vision blurred. She swallowed hard, willing herself to keep her breathing steady. No matter how many times she told herself she was past this, the sting still found a way in.

Then another voice cut through the air.

"What has Sienna ever done to you, anyway?" Logan stood a few feet away, arms relaxed but shoulders squared. His tone wasn't loud. It wasn't aggressive. Just steady. Intentional.

"You've been stuck in her past since the day she started here," he said. "But she's here. She's doing the work. What exactly is your problem?"

Elena blinked, caught off guard. "I wasn't talking to her."

Logan let out a short, humorless laugh. "I know. You never talk directly to the people you enjoy tearing down."

Silence stretched between them. Sienna fought to keep her breathing even.

Elena's eyes narrowed. "I was just saying—"

"No," Logan said, voice firmer now. "You were just making sure everyone else keeps seeing Sienna the way *you* want them to. Like she's still stuck in the past she worked hard to leave behind."

A muscle in Elena's jaw twitched. "People don't change. She'll always be one step away from losing it."

Logan exhaled, shaking his head. "What are you really trying to do? Are you covering up something in your own past by making such a big deal about others?"

Before Elena could respond, another voice cut through the tension.

"Elena."

Maiya stood at the edge of the work area with Drew beside her, arms at her sides, gaze steady. Not angry—just... tired.

Elena turned, her expression shifting from defensive to unreadable.

"We need to speak with you," Maiya said.

Drew gestured toward the supply room. "Privately."

Elena hesitated for a half-second before scoffing. "Fine." Without another word, she followed them, the door clicking shut behind them.

She crossed her arms and leaned against a shelf of paint cans. "What is this, an intervention?"

Maiya's lips pressed together. "You've made it clear you have opinions about who belongs here. But this isn't *your* project, Elena. It belongs to the whole community."

Drew's voice was calm, measured. "And you've spent a lot of

time making sure people feel like they *don't* belong."

Elena scoffed. "Oh, come on. You're acting like I'm out to ruin lives. I was just—"

"You were just making sure everyone knows you don't believe people can change," Maiya interrupted. "And that's a problem."

Elena crossed her arms tighter. "It's not my fault I pay attention. I remember things. That's not a crime."

Drew studied her for a long moment. "You keep saying people don't change. But are *you* willing to?"

Elena scoffed again.

"That's interesting," Drew said quietly. "Because from where I'm standing, the only person who keeps making sure everyone stays in their past... is you."

Elena let out a short laugh, but it wasn't convincing. "You're overreacting. People talk about each other all the time. It's not like I'm making things up."

Maiya shook her head. "It's not about whether it happened. It's about the way you use it."

Elena's mouth pressed into a tight line. "I don't see why this is suddenly a big deal. Sienna's fine. She's got Logan rushing to her defense, so clearly, she doesn't need my approval."

Drew's voice didn't rise, but there was steel in it now. "That's not the point, and you know it. You're tearing people down to make yourself feel better. And if that's the only way you know how to belong here... maybe you need to ask yourself why."

Silence.

Elena looked away. Her fingers tightened around her arms. For a moment, it looked like she might argue.

But then she huffed and shifted on her feet. "Whatever. I don't have time for this."

She turned on her heel and walked out.

Drew watched her go, then turned to Maiya. "That won't be the last of it."

Maiya exhaled slowly. "No. But maybe it's the first time she's actually listening."

They stepped back into the main room, and the air still felt tight, like a balloon stretched to its limit.

Maiya took a slow look around, her gaze sweeping over the volunteers—some of whom had nodded along or stayed silent when they knew better.

She took a breath. "This stops right now."

A few people shifted uncomfortably.

Her eyes landed on one specific volunteer—someone who had helped spread Elena's words earlier that week.

Her voice sharpened. "*Period.*"

The volunteer swallowed hard and turned quickly back to their work.

Satisfied, Maiya exhaled, then scanned the room until she found Sienna.

Sienna had set her roller aside, wiping her hands with a rag. She felt... raw. Exposed. Like she'd just been shoved under a spotlight she hadn't asked for.

Maiya stepped over and hesitated before speaking. "Hey. You okay?"

Sienna glanced toward the door where Elena had disappeared. "I don't know."

Maiya nodded, quiet understanding in her eyes. "I meant what I said, you know. You *belong* here."

Sienna swallowed. "I thought I did. But some people can't see who I am or what I've done to get here. No matter what I do, my past is always waiting in someone else's words."

Maiya's expression softened. "You most definitely belong here. I should've said something sooner. But understand this—we're not going to let that behavior continue. It stops. Or *she* goes."

Sienna looked down, exhaling slowly. The weight in her chest didn't disappear, but it shifted—just a little.

"Thanks."

Maiya gave her a small, sure smile. "You ever need to talk, you know where to find me."

And just like that, the moment passed.

But something had changed.

For the first time, Sienna wasn't the only one fighting her past.

Someone else had stepped in.

And maybe—just maybe—she didn't have to fight it alone.

SARAH'S WISDOM

The sunset this evening was truly remarkable. As Sienna admires the vibrant orange, purple, and red streaks in the evening sky, she is transported back to Granny's porch. She and Granny had witnessed many equally spectacular sunsets together, sitting side by side with their hands wrapped around warm cups of tea. Now Granny is no longer around—watching sunsets from heaven—and that absence in Sienna's life feels particularly burdensome.

Despite Elena's words, Logan's support, and Maiya and Drew standing up for her, she has managed to get through the day. But as things are winding down, the weight of it all is beginning to catch up with her. She doesn't feel quite ready to go home yet. So, she decides to stop by the bookstore.

Sarah notices immediately that Sienna looks exhausted, both physically and emotionally.

"Hello, Sienna," Sarah greets with a warm and welcoming voice. "Can I get you something? Perhaps some coffee or tea?"

Sienna hesitates, noting that Sarah has never offered her tea before. Intrigued, she asks, "What kind of tea do you have?"

Sarah responds with a smile, "We have regular orange pekoe, Earl Grey, and a really nice mint chamomile blend."

Sienna's breath catches—"mint chamomile," she whispers.
A flood of memories rushes back to Sienna—warm summer nights on Granny's porch, the aroma of mint and honey lingering in the air, Granny's soothing voice narrating stories as they watched the sky transition into twilight. Her fingers instinctively curl against

the counter, anchoring herself. It's the same brand. That wasn't just any tea—that was Granny's tea.

"I would love a cup of mint chamomile, please," Sienna says, her voice now softer. "It's the flavor Granny and I shared during my visits."

Sarah senses something deeper in Sienna's tone. She prepares two cups, fills them with hot water, and then inquires, "Would you like some honey with it?"

Sienna blinks. That was exactly how Granny always prepared it. She swallows hard, a small but appreciative smile appearing on her face. "Yes, I would love that."

Sarah hands a cup to Sienna before settling in across from her. "It's my favorite as well, especially at the end of the day."

Sienna gazes down at her cup, breathing in the familiar fragrance. A profound ache settles in her chest.

"Days like today make me miss her more than usual," she expresses, yearning to hear Granny's comforting words that assured her of her strength. But after everything with Elena, her confidence is shaken.

Sarah doesn't probe. She simply waits, allowing the conversation to unfold naturally.

Sienna traces her finger along the rim of the cup. "Granny had a way about her," she reflects softly. "She always made me feel safe. Like I mattered. She was the one person who never gave up on me." Her throat tightens. "She's the one who connected me with the woman who guided me to rehab."

Sarah stirs her tea, her expression contemplative. "I wouldn't have guessed."

Sienna exhales, running a finger along the rim of her cup. "Yes. Not one of the better times in my life."

Sarah tilts her head. "You carry yourself like someone who has fought hard to reach where they are. You seem quite grounded."

Sienna's composure wavers. Granny used to say that. *You're stronger than you think, sweetheart.* Her grip on the cup tightens.

Sarah notices. "She believed in you, didn't she?"

Sienna releases a shaky breath and nods. "More than I did." She peers into her tea, her voice lowering. "I want to believe I've changed. But what if... what if I haven't?"

Sarah sets her cup down and meets Sienna's gaze. Sienna hesitates, grappling with her uncertainty.

"Elena acts as though I'm deluding myself," she confesses. "As if at any moment, I'll regress to who I used to be." She swallows hard. "And maybe she's right."

"Oh, Sienna, why do you think that?" Sarah inquires, her tone gentle yet resolute. She leans in slightly, offering words of wisdom. "You don't need to prove anything to anyone but yourself, especially not to those who have already formed their opinions," Sarah states. "But you can continue proving to yourself that you are moving forward."

Sienna swallows, averting her gaze. "I thought I was."

Sarah allows a moment of silence before responding. "And you still are. Progress isn't about never facing challenges again, Sienna. It's about how many times you choose not to revert back."

Sienna exhales slowly, peering into her cup. "Granny would say the same thing."

Sarah smiles tenderly. "She sounds like she was a remarkable and wise woman."

"She was," Sienna whispers. "The best."

For the next hour, Sienna pours out her emotions. She delves into her financial hardships, the journey through rehab, the distance she has traveled, and the fragility she currently feels. She opens up about Elena's constant criticism, the weight of her words, and the creeping fear that perhaps, just perhaps, she hasn't evolved at all.

Sarah listens intently—truly listens. She refrains from offering empty reassurances or hastily dismissing Sienna's concerns. Instead, she sits with her, embracing the moment.

When Sienna finally eases back in her chair, exhausted yet somewhat relieved, Sarah refills their tea. Sienna has shared before. With therapists. With individuals who pose the right questions but never quite understand her. Yet, this feels different. It's natural. It's... necessary.

"I'm not even sure why I'm confiding all of this in you," Sienna muses.

Sarah smiles, stirring her tea. "Perhaps because you needed to."

Sienna lets out a small, lighter laugh this time. Not tinged with bitterness. Just weariness. Just... a sense of relief. For the first time that day, she isn't shouldering it all alone.

FIRM FOUNDATION

It was 7 a.m., and Maiya and Drew were already making their rounds at the community center, going through their punch list. The grand opening was just three weeks away, and each task needed a volunteer assigned and the right supplies on hand to finish on time.

Maiya glanced around at the progress, her heart swelling with excitement. "It seems like just yesterday when I was at that planning board meeting," she said to Drew. "The transformation is amazing. We're so close."

Drew nodded, scanning the site with a sense of pride. "You've done an excellent job, and you've come so far. We can see the end a bit clearer now. Everyone has a sense of pride in what we've built —not just the building, but the volunteers, too. People have grown through this project."

Maiya smiled. She pushed aside the thought—there was still work to be done, she reminded herself. "Okay, we have our list of tasks and volunteer assignments for the meeting today. Let's see how we stand with supplies."

"There's another shipment due at 9, right after the meeting," Drew added as they walked toward the supply room. "Let's check what's left in there."

As they approached, two volunteers walked out, shaking their heads and exchanging uncomfortable glances. Maiya and Drew came from one direction, and Logan approached from another. Before they even stepped inside, they heard Elena's voice again.

"Honestly, I don't see how someone like Logan will ever hold down a steady job. He won't have the protection of Maiya and Drew once he leaves here."

Maiya's jaw clenched, but before she could say anything, Logan gestured for them to wait.

"Let me handle this," he said.

Drew and Maiya exchanged a glance, hesitating, then nodded in agreement, stepping aside.

Logan walked into the supply room, and the conversation stopped immediately. He let the silence hang for a moment before speaking.

"Good morning!" he said, flashing a knowing smile. "How are you two on this wonderful day?"

He signed the volunteer log, moving at an unhurried pace toward the door. Then, without looking back, he added, "Three more weeks, and I won't have to hear your half-truths anymore. I used to believe people like you. Not anymore."

With that, he walked out, winking at Drew and Maiya as he passed them in the hallway.

"All yours," he whispered.

Drew and Maiya entered the supply room casually, acting as if nothing had happened.

"Elena," Maiya said, making her jump slightly. "Do you have the list of supplies on hand?"

Elena quickly recovered, handing Maiya the clipboard. "Yes, here it is," she said.

Drew folded his arms. "You're aware the next shipment is due at 9, right?"

"Yes, Drew. After the meeting, right?" she responded, nodding.

Drew and Maiya exchanged another glance but said nothing more. As they left the supply room, Maiya's voice was tight with frustration.

"I told Elena she had to stop, or she was out. She's targeting Logan now—enough is enough. She can't even pretend to follow the rules, not even with three weeks left. This is coming to a head, and it won't benefit anyone."

Drew sighed, knowing she was right.

"After today's meeting, let's make her the last person assigned," Maiya added.

Drew nodded. It was time.

At 8 a.m., volunteers gathered, the energy in the room buzzing as the final push toward the grand opening loomed.

Maiya stepped forward. "First, I want to thank all of you for the work you've put in. We're three weeks away from something incredible. You should all be very proud of what we have accomplished."

Drew chimed in. "We've reviewed everything left to do. Going forward, we'll be in the supply room each morning as you sign in. We'll go over assignments and make sure you have what you need. We're going to start that today—painters first, then cleaners, then anyone without an assignment, and finally, supplies and distribution."

Maiya paused, scanning the room. "One last thing—I know these last few weeks can be stressful. But please, let's keep showing each other kindness and respect. We're building more than just a center—we're building a community."

Her tone was firm but vague. She didn't call Elena out directly, but everyone in the room understood.

"Now, let's get to work."

One by one, the volunteers filtered through the line. Eventually, only Elena and Sienna remained.

Elena glanced at Sienna. "I thought you were a painter. Why haven't you been assigned?"

Sienna gave a small smile. "My project is finished. Today's my last day—I have a new job."

Elena tilted her head and let out one of her infamous knowing "Ohs."

Sienna, having had enough, took a deep breath.

"Elena, I understand that you think you're better than me because I did rehab. That just makes you different. I don't know what struggles life has brought your way or from what age, but whatever they were, they made you a mean, judgmental, manipulative person. In my eyes, that is not better."

"Yes, I've made bad choices, but I continue to work to correct them. To be a better person. NOT for YOU, but for ME. I hope someday—and preferably someday soon—you will be able to see that you need to change. When you see that, and we meet again, I hope you can see me as I am, not as I once was. I wish you all the best."

As she finished, Maiya called Elena in for her turn.

Elena's lips parted slightly, as if she might respond, but then she pressed them into a thin line. Without a word, she straightened her shoulders and walked forward.

Elena walked in confidently, assuming she'd be given her usual assignment. She expected to be told to handle the supply shipment.

But as she looked at Drew and Maiya, she immediately sensed something was off.

Maiya started. "Elena, first, I want to thank you for the work you've done in the supply room. You've kept it organized, and you've been great at tracking inventory."

Elena smiled, soaking in the praise.

Then Maiya's voice shifted. "A few weeks ago, I told you that gossip about other volunteers had to stop. This morning, we heard you again. Even Logan heard you—and in his own way, he addressed it. I'm sorry you haven't taken my instruction to heart." Maiya's eyes met hers. "Elena, we've built more than a building here—we've built a community, a team. And that team needs to trust one another. This morning, when we heard you breaking that trust once again, I realized that we can't allow you to continue here. Please turn in your volunteer badge and gather your things.

Drew will walk you out."

Elena's jaw dropped. "You're joking, right? There's still work to do."

Drew shook his head. "The work will get done, but not with your judgment weighing people down. Elena, you're capable of more than this—you just don't see it yet. I truly hope and pray that someday you do. But for now, this is where we part ways."

Elena's face hardened. Without another word, she gathered her things and walked out, Drew following behind.

The door clicked shut behind Elena. Drew let out a quiet breath before turning to Sienna.

"So, today's your last day," he said.

Maiya gave a small smile. "You've done a lot here, Sienna. We appreciate it."

Sienna nodded. "I've learned a lot too."

Maiya glanced at the clock. "We've got a supply delivery coming in soon. Any chance you can stay a little longer to help organize it?"

Sienna hesitated for just a second, then nodded. "Yeah, I can do that."

Drew grinned. "Knew we could count on you."

With that, Sienna rolled up her sleeves and got to work one last time.

ACKNOWLEDGED GROWTH

Logan took a sip of his coffee, feeling the weight of two different futures pressing down on him. He had lined up the construction crew job a few weeks ago, knowing the community center work was ending. It was steady, secure, and a sure thing. And yet... he couldn't shake the thought of Mitch's offer from a couple of days ago.

Drew leaned against the counter, studying Logan's expression. "You look like a guy trying to solve a puzzle without all the pieces."

Sarah smiled. "That's his 'thinking too hard' face."

Logan exhaled. "I've got two job offers on the table. I need to figure out which one to take."

Drew raised an eyebrow. "Mitch's apprenticeship and...?"

"A construction crew. Entry-level, but decent pay, steady work. I set it up a few weeks ago, knowing I'd need something soon."

Sarah nodded. "Alright, let's break it down. What's the best thing about the construction job?"

"The money is about the same," he said finally. "But the construction job has better benefits—health insurance, 401(k), the whole package. It's a big company, one of many in the area. They're always busy."

Drew nodded. "Sounds solid. What's the downside?"

Logan leaned back. "First in, first out. If work slows, I'm gone before the guys who've been there longer. And in construction, things dry up fast sometimes."

Sarah sipped her coffee. "And Mitch's?"

Logan exhaled. "No benefits, at least not yet. If work dries up, I don't have a safety net. But I've been thinking..." He hesitated before continuing. "Mitch only does so much because he's just one guy. If I help him grow the business, maybe we don't have to worry about slow seasons as much."

Drew's eyebrows lifted slightly. "That's a significant thought, Logan."

"Yeah, but that's another risk, right?" Logan ran a hand through his hair. "Mitch worries about spreading himself too thin. He doesn't take on more because he doesn't want to overextend. But if the economy shifts and work slows, how do we keep it going?"

Sarah smiled slightly. "Sounds like something Mitch could guide you through."

Logan nodded. "That's the thing—he's been in business for years. He's seen the ups and downs, survived all of them. If I take the apprenticeship, I wouldn't just be learning a trade—I'd be learning how to keep a business running."

Drew tapped a finger against the table. "So, it comes down to this—do you want to work for a company that controls your future, or help build something where you have control?"

Logan sat with that for a long moment. "That's exactly it."

Sarah leaned forward. "Then it's time to see what Mitch thinks about all this. Because if you're going to take this seriously, you need to know if he's willing to teach you that side of things too."

Drew shrugged. "You've got one more step besides that—get Mitch's offer in writing. If you're going to make a long-term decision, you need all the details."

Logan nodded slowly. "Yeah. I guess it's time to talk to him."

Mitch looked up from his workbench as Logan stepped into the shop. A slow, approving nod formed as he set down his measuring tape.

"Didn't expect you back this soon," he said, leaning against the counter.

Logan smirked slightly. "Figured I should get this sorted while I still have options."

Mitch wiped his hands on a rag and crossed his arms. "That a good sign or a bad one?"

"Depends," Logan admitted. He glanced around the shop, then back at Mitch. "I've been thinking about what this really means—the work, the business, the future. And I've got questions."

Mitch raised a brow, intrigued. "Alright. Let's hear 'em."

Logan hesitated for just a second. "You've been at this a long time. You know how to run a business, keep work steady, and make sure things don't fall apart. We've talked about what you expect from me and, to a certain extent, what I can expect from you. But let's flip this for a second—if you were me and I were you, knowing what you know now after years in this business, what questions would you ask?"

Mitch studied him for a moment, measuring his words.

Logan continued, a small smirk forming. "And I don't just mean the mechanics—like how to install a door in a house that's settled wrong." He let the words hang there, knowing Mitch would catch the reference.

Mitch huffed a quiet laugh. "Yeah, glad we got through that!"

"Me too," Logan admitted. "But that's my point. I know there's a whole lot more to this than just learning how to frame a wall or fix an uneven door. I appreciate your offer, and I want to make the best decision for both of us. But there's a lot about apprenticeship and running a business that I don't even know to ask about. So, tell me—what should I be asking?"

Mitch rubbed his jaw, the hint of a smirk appearing.

"You're asking the right question, kid. Grab a seat. Let's talk." Mitch gestured to a stool while he grabbed a folder from his workbench. He slid it across the table. "Here's what I put together," he said. "It's not complicated. It lays out what I'd expect from you, how pay increases as you take on more responsibility, and what the long-term plan looks like."

Logan flipped through the pages, scanning the breakdown. He wasn't great with paperwork, but it was clear enough—structured, realistic, and thorough.

Mitch continued, "You'd start as an apprentice, just like we talked about. Learn every part of the trade—not just the hands-on work, but how to handle permits, order materials, and bid on jobs. As you take on more, I'll pull back. If things go the way I think they will, you'll be running jobs on your own within a few years. If all works out, in about ten years—maybe less, depending on my health—I'd step away, and the business would be yours."

Logan nodded, absorbing the plan. It made sense. The numbers, the structure, the future Mitch was laying out. But still... something didn't sit right. He hesitated, then looked up.

"Mitch, you've worked with a lot of guys over the years. Why now? Why me?"

Mitch exhaled, rubbing his jaw before answering. "I'm not getting any younger, kid. I could just let the business dry up, pick up odd jobs here and there, and coast into retirement. Or I could pass along what I've built." He met Logan's gaze, his expression serious but not soft. "You and I have had our moments. You know that. But you've got the same grit and determination I had at your age. You don't just work hard—you work smart. You learn fast, and once you learn something, you don't need to be told twice. That's rare."

Logan absorbed that, unsure how to respond.

"If you commit to working with me for ten years—or less, depending on how things go—you'll have most of the knowledge I've built over a lifetime. Your skills show me you're a natural at this, but more than that, I've seen how much you've grown. I wouldn't make this offer if I didn't think you could handle it. I'd be honored if you'd take it." Mitch let the moment settle, then smirked. "As long as you don't get a swelled head about it."

Logan huffed a small laugh. He looked down at the papers, running his fingers over the edge of the folder.

Mitch leaned forward, his tone turning practical again. "That's a lot to take in. A ten-year commitment is not something to take lightly. Take this, read it through a few times, and then get back to me. You don't have to decide today, but don't just think about what's easy now. Think about where you want to be in ten years."

Logan met his gaze and nodded. "A few days should be enough." He tucked the folder under his arm and stood. For the first time in a long time, he wasn't just looking for a way out of a tough situation. He was looking at a way forward. And this time, he wasn't waiting for someone else to tell him what to do—he was choosing it for himself.

GRAND OPENING

The newly completed community center stood proud in the morning sun, casting long shadows that highlighted the fresh paint and crisp banners. Volunteers bustled about, setting up chairs, arranging refreshments, and making last-minute adjustments, filling the air with the hum of conversation and laughter—a stark contrast to the silence that once pervaded the empty building.

Maiya stood near the entrance, holding the notes for her speech, though she knew she wouldn't use them. She took a deep breath to center herself. Six months ago, this place had been a dilapidated structure, but now it stood as a testament to resilience, community, and second chances.

Drew approached with a smile. "Nervous?"

"A bit," Maiya admitted. "But mostly grateful."

Drew nodded. "You should be. You brought this to life."

Maiya shook her head. "We all did."

When she stepped to the podium, the crowd quieted. She gazed out at the familiar faces—individuals who had worked tirelessly, debated, reconciled, and evolved together.

"Six months ago, we stood in front of a building that seemed impossible to restore," she began. "We saw crumbling walls, peeling paint, and an extensive list of obstacles. But more importantly, we saw a need. A need for a space where people could gather, heal, and grow." Her gaze swept across the crowd. "And now, thanks to each of you, that vision is a reality."

The audience burst into applause. Maiya thanked them for their hard work, dedication, and patience. She closed with a line that carried more weight than the walls themselves:

"This isn't just a building. It's a reflection of the people who restored it."

Then she gestured toward Drew. "And I know someone else who has a few words to share."

Drew chuckled as he took the microphone. "You all know I'm not one for long speeches, so I'll keep this brief. What we accomplished here is more than wood and drywall. It's about people. About showing up when it's difficult. About choosing to believe that something broken can be renewed."

His eyes briefly met Logan's in the crowd. "And that's not just true for buildings. It's true for us, too."

Applause followed as the ribbon-cutting ceremony began. Laughter and cheers filled the air as the doors officially opened.

Later, as the event wound down, Maiya scanned the room for Elena, whom she had seen earlier near the back. She had already slipped out. Still, Maiya was glad Elena had come. Maybe today had stirred something in her. Maybe she was beginning to see the rebuilding needed in her own life. Whether that spark would ignite change remained to be seen.

As people began filtering inside, Maiya found Keith standing slightly apart, watching everything with a contemplative expression.

"You should have been up there with us," she said.

Keith shook his head. "No. This was your project. You made it happen."

Maiya offered a warm smile. "I just want to thank you—for everything you've done, and for continuing to support the center. It means more than you know."

Keith exhaled, rubbing the back of his neck. "I didn't do it for recognition."

"I know," she replied. "And that's exactly why it matters."

Keith said nothing at first. He watched the volunteers and guests circulating through the new space. Then he gave a slow nod, eyes sweeping the room.

"It took longer than I ever expected," he said quietly, **"but it's what I always hoped it would be."**

Nearby, Sienna stood near the entrance, watching the crowd with a pensive expression. She had known this day would come— but now that it had, leaving felt... strange.

Sarah approached, holding two cups of tea. "Chamomile?"

Sienna accepted the cup with a soft laugh. "Perfect. Thanks."

"Congratulations on the promotion! Day shift now, right?"

Sienna exhaled and nodded. "Yeah. It's a step up. More stability. More responsibility."

Sarah studied her. "Are you ready?"

Sienna considered. A few months ago, she might have hesitated—let the past hold her back. But not now.

"I think I am."

Sarah smiled. "I know you are."

They stood quietly for a moment before Sienna added, "This place... it's different than I expected. I came here thinking I had to prove something. To show people I wasn't who I used to be. But somewhere along the way, I stopped needing to prove it. I just... realized who I really am. And that the past doesn't define me anymore."

Sarah nodded, a knowing look in her eyes. "That's how real change works."

Sienna smiled. "Yeah. I suppose it is."

Later, as the event neared its conclusion, Logan found Drew,

Sarah, and Maiya near the back of the room. He hesitated for only a moment before stepping forward.

"I've made my decision," he said, looking at Drew and Sarah. "I've accepted Mitch's offer."

Drew nodded, a proud but measured look on his face. "A good choice."

Sarah grinned. "Not just a job—a future. Congratulations, Logan! I'm really happy for you."

Maiya crossed her arms, smirking. "Me too. I knew it. You don't invest this much time in a project just to walk away from building things."

Logan chuckled. "I guess not."

Drew placed a hand on his shoulder. "You'll do well, Logan."

"And if things get tough," Logan said, "I know where to find you."

Drew nodded. "Exactly."

As the event wound down, Drew, Sarah, and Maiya found a quiet moment together—fittingly, near the coffee station.

"We've got the basics covered," Drew said. "Keith's managing the building, and a small team of volunteers is running the calendar and outreach. Sarah's heading the new coffee room and children's story room, and we've got a few others stepping into part-time roles until long-term hires are in place."

Maiya nodded. "It's not perfect yet, but it's functional. And it's in good hands."

Sarah smiled. "I might spend more time back at the bookstore, but I'll be here too—especially in the story room. Being around kids feels like a blessing I didn't expect at this stage."

Maiya exhaled, glancing back at the center. "I'll be sticking around too. There are grants to apply for, programs to launch. The renovation was just the beginning—now it has to thrive."

Drew smirked. "I knew you wouldn't walk away."

She chuckled. "This place has a way of drawing you back in."

As Logan looked around the bustling center, he realized something important. This wasn't just about work.

It was about belonging.

And for the first time, he wasn't looking for a way out—he had found a place to stay.

The doors of the center remained open long after the speeches ended. And as sunlight streamed in and people came and went, one quiet truth settled over them all:

This was never just about rebuilding a place.

It was about rebuilding people.

AFTERWORD

Personal Reflection

What we say and do is closely observed—and, more importantly, remembered—by the people around us. Our lives are witnessed by those who know and love us, by coworkers, by strangers we encounter in passing. We are observed by fellow believers in Jesus, by Christians who have been hurt by other Christians, by those who are curious about Him, by people who have wandered and are searching, by the enemy of our souls—and most importantly, by Jesus Himself, my Lord and Savior, who died on the cross for every word, thought, and action that fails to bring Him glory.

This book was prompted by something someone close to me once said:

"Christians scare me."

Oh, the pain in those words. Jesus told us to love one another and to shine as lights in a dark world.

So how can we represent Jesus well when our words and actions inspire fear instead of offering hope?

Should there be fear? Yes—**a reverent fear** of facing eternity without God. But fear of *Christians*? No. Those who follow Jesus should reflect His love, His character, and His willingness to lay down His life for us.

To those who have witnessed the imperfections in us—and especially in me—I offer my sincere apologies. I pray the Holy Spirit helps me become more sensitive to His voice, more responsive to His promptings, and more faithful in being a witness rather than a stumbling block.

I am far from perfect. But I trust that through the Spirit's work and the sacrifice of Jesus, I am being made new. My prayer is that my words and actions would bring glory to God. And to those who observe my life, I humbly ask for grace—and for gentle reminders when I falter. I am a work in progress. But with the strength I receive from Christ, I believe I can keep moving forward.

And to you, the reader—thank you. If you've read this far, I hope you'll pause and pray. Ask God how the Holy Spirit might be speaking to you through this story. Reflect on how we, as followers of Jesus, can better reflect His heart—through our thoughts, our words, and our actions.

Then, with a grateful heart, step out into the world—not as someone trying to be perfect, but as someone who points to the One who is.

Live as a faithful witness. And remember: it is only by God's grace that any of us are able to do so.

OTHER BOOKS BY THE AUTHOR

Pray Daily: A Practical Approach to a Powerful Prayer Life

https://amzn.to/4kaBJ71

Do you desire a stronger, more consistent prayer life? Are you looking for a structured way to deepen your faith with guided prayer and reflection?

Transform your prayer life in just six weeks! A practical, learn to pray book, *Pray Daily* is a 6-week faith-based instructional workbook designed to help you build a meaningful prayer habit through guided prayer prompts, a daily prayer planner and a structured prayer log. Whether you're new to prayer or looking to grow spiritually, this learn how to pray book will guide you step by step.

Weekly Prayer Planner

https://amzn.to/3GUpUDm

The *Weekly Prayer Planner* is a 54-week, UNDATED, Christian planner with weekly Bible verses, Prayer Request tracking and space to reflect. Stay spiritually grounded while keeping life organized with this beautifully designed undated 54-week planner. It was created for Christian women, men, or teens to help you stay focused on your priorities, both practical and prayerful, all year long.

The two-page layout includes a different Bible verse each week to center your thoughts and guide you. The week has an ample display with Sunday through Wednesday on the top left, Thursday through Saturday on the right, plus a full width area at the bottom of each week to record prayer requests and when prayers are answered.

Prayer Log

https://amzn.to/4IU8Ihp

The *Prayer Log* is designed as a companion book to *Pray Daily* to help you track your prayers in one place, making it easy to see prayer requests and answered prayers at a glance. By regularly recording your prayers and the answer, the log is a reminder of God's faithfulness, encouraging you to pray with purpose and expectancy.

The *Prayer Log* shows at a glance which prayers need continued focus, allowing you to shift to praise when prayers are answered. Since some prayers take longer for answers to be seen, the log helps you quickly identify prayers that have been answered without flipping through multiple planner pages and journal entries.

ABOUT THE AUTHOR

Mary Cross never planned to become an author. She has served on many prayer teams and often prays aloud in group settings. During retirement, she felt led to share practical tools to help others grow in their relationship with God. That led to *Pray Daily: A Practical Approach to a Powerful Prayer Life*, a six-week workbook for building a steady prayer habit. Shortly after that was published, a conversation with someone afraid of Christians inspired her next book, *Rising from the Ruins: A Story of Restoration and Healing*—a reflection on how our lives speak to those around us, especially when our actions fall short of our beliefs.

In addition to her prayer books, she has created planners, journals, and other practical tools. Her writing remains focused on one thing: following God's leading and offering encouragement where she can. She now lives in Central Florida with her husband of nearly 49 years.

www.ingramcontent.com/pod-product-compliance
Lightning Source LLC
Chambersburg PA
CBHW071330130626
46556CB00004B/1826